Chronos Fade

By

Dr. Shabina Sheth

Chronos Fade

Author: Dr. Shabina Sheth

Publisher: Self-published by Dr. Shabinabegam Abdul Majid Sheth (Dr. Shabina Sheth)

ISBN: [978-93-343-7690-6]

Printed in various locations worldwide based on the platform's print-on-demand services.

Cover Design by **Dr. Shabinabegam Abdul Majid Sheth**

For permissions or inquiries, contact: dr.shabinasheth@gmail.com

Dedication

To my little explorer, Muhammed Khizar — may you always see the magic hidden in cracks, questions, and quiet moments.

And

To those who have stared at a crack in reality and wondered if it stared back — this is for you.

Contents

Chapter 1: The Obsession

The air in Alistair Finch's office was stale in a way that clung to your clothes — paper dust, cold coffee, maybe even the faint tang of old glue from bindings that had been cracked open a hundred times. The window glass wore a film of grime that no cloth could really erase, and the light that slipped through was a thin, reluctant shaft, catching dust motes mid-dance.

Stacks of journals leaned at dangerous angles, dictionaries fat with the weight of dead tongues sat like patient tombstones. Somewhere under it all, his desktop hummed in that low, persistent way that became part of the furniture of his mind.

At forty-two, Finch was all edges — face, voice, thoughts — and whatever softness had once been in his eyes had been replaced by the dull shine of obsession. He hadn't shaved. He'd forgotten to eat. A mug of tea sat beside the keyboard, the kind of brown that only happens after hours of neglect, surface crinkled with a skin.

A pen twirled between his fingers — habit, tic, maybe both — as his gaze fixed on the spread before him. Laminated photographs. Years of exile distilled into a handful of images: strange carved marks from an Andean cave no one had cared enough to study properly. Not hieroglyphs. Not cuneiform. Not even a cousin of anything in the known family of language.

They'd been called scratches. Accidents of geology. The sort of thing archaeologists wave away with a smile before moving on to the "real" find. But he'd felt something when he first saw them, like a tiny electrical shiver running under the skin. A phrase had risen in his mind, uninvited: *to cleanse... to prepare.* No idea why.

His colleagues had laughed — kindly, at first, then less so — right up until the grant money dried up and the invitations stopped coming. He'd said the marks were a meta-syntax older than humans themselves, a structure that shaped thought the way gravity shapes rivers. No one listened.

That loss — the career, the friends — it hurt, but it wasn't the wound that drove him. The real wound sat in a cheap frame at the edge of his desk. A woman's face. Warm eyes, the kind that made you believe in kindness itself. His mother.

Alzheimer's had stolen her slowly. The way a candle gutters, not in one dramatic puff but in a series of uneven flickers. He remembered holding her hand in the nursing home, skin like tissue paper, her gaze fixed somewhere far away. He'd wanted to shake her, to say, *It's me, Mum,* as if sheer insistence could pull her back. That was when memory — and the architecture that held it together — became his religion.

And then there was Sarah. He didn't think about Sarah. Not if he could help it. When he did, it was just sound and smell: tyres screaming, glass shattering, a sweetness in the air that didn't belong. He buried that memory deep.

Weeks of sleepless nights had narrowed to one sequence of glyphs that refused to yield. Coffee, cold air through the cracked window, muttering to himself like a man who'd been too long without company. Then, at 3:17 in the morning, something shifted. Not meaning. Pattern. Like a vibration under the words. A hum.

It wasn't to be read. It was to be switched on.

Now, twelve hours later, the algorithm he'd built was ready. Lines of code flickered on the screen, his hands hovering. Then — click.

The screen blazed green and blue, characters tumbling too fast to follow, the hum of the machine deepening until it seemed to live in his bones. And then — nothing. Just one glyph in the centre, pulsing, faintly warm.

No revelation. No lightning bolt. Just disappointment.

He stood, bones creaking, and went to the window. The street outside was half-lit, the hour between night and morning. Same old brownstones. Same old oak tree at the corner — except... it wasn't leaning anymore. Perfectly straight now, every branch symmetrical. Too symmetrical.

A trick of the eyes, he told himself.

He reached for his battered copy of *Syntactic Structures*. Only it wasn't battered. It wasn't blue. It was green. And the title — *Grammar and the Mind.*

Cold spread through him. Page after page confirmed it: Chomsky's name, but not Chomsky's book.

The oak tree. The book. What else?

His phone was suddenly heavy in his hand. A search for the original cover brought up nothing but blue. Blue, blue, blue.

In his hand: green.

A tremor started in his fingers and crawled up his arms. This wasn't exhaustion. This wasn't a trick.

Alistair Finch, who had devoted his life to preserving memory, had just felt the first thin slice of it slip sideways. The Chronos Fade had begun. And it had chosen a book as its opening whisper.

Chapter 2: Subtle Anomalies

The glyph pulsed on his screen. Slow. Patient. Like it knew something he didn't.

Alistair just sat there, eyes fixed, stomach tightening the way it does when you realise you might have made a terrible mistake. He'd activated it. He was sure. The pattern. The key. And now...

The hairs on his arms lifted. He started tapping his fingers against the desk — not thinking about it, just needing to let the static out somehow. A sharp breath. He told himself to focus. To stay here, in this room. But the world had a way of warping at the edges now. He muttered to himself, the kind of mumbling you do when there's no one left to hear.

The next hour turned into something like a ritual. Books off shelves. Covers, titles, publication dates — checked against his notes, his backups, his own memory. Most matched. Some didn't. Not in ways anyone else would notice, but enough to make his skin prickle: a publisher logo he'd never seen, a different subtitle, a dedication to a stranger.

Then his music collection. A Brahms symphony — same scuff on the jewel case, but a conductor's name he didn't know. His photo archive — there, a holiday shot from five years back. But now there was a tiny café in the corner, white awning, handwritten menu board, a place he was certain hadn't existed when he pressed the shutter.

He tried to explain it away. Misprints. Limited editions. Tricks of the light. Maybe a prank, though how anyone could alter a shelf of books, a pile of CDs, and digital files all at once was beyond him.

The only constant was the hum of his computer and that quiet glow from the glyph, which seemed to warm — just slightly — whenever he spotted something wrong. As though it noticed.

He forced himself into the shower. Cold water. Hard. It didn't wash the fog out of his head. Dressing felt mechanical, his limbs stiff, like someone else was pulling the strings. Coffee, he thought. Always coffee.

The mug he reached for was his favourite — big, chipped, ridiculous. Bought it in Kyoto at the Global Linguistics Summit in 2015, laughing with Ben Carter over how hideous it was. He could still hear Ben's laugh.

But the logo was different. Totally different. The chip was in the same place, but the words read *Cognitive Semantics Symposium*. New design. Same mug.

The coffee slopped over the counter when his hand shook. The burn jolted him, but only for a second.

"No," he whispered. It came out rough, almost cracked. "No, no, no..."

The mug hit the counter hard, the sound echoing too loudly in the stillness. His chest felt tight. Breathing was work.

He needed an anchor. Something — someone — outside himself. Evelyn Reed. She remembered everything. If the world was changing, she'd see it.

He called.

"Evelyn?... it's Alistair. I— I have a question."

Her voice was crisp, reassuring. "It's early for you. Another glyph breakthrough?"

"Something like that. Do you remember Kyoto? 2015? The awful oversized mugs—"

Pause. "Kyoto? Alistair, there was no Kyoto summit in 2015. That was Berlin. *Cognitive Semantics Symposium*. I still have my mug."

The blood seemed to drain out of him. Berlin. She kept talking, but all he could hear was the spring wind in Kyoto, the ramen shop, the cherry blossoms. Arguing grammar over lukewarm sake. The green lanyards.

"You're sure?" His voice barely made it out.

"Of course. Kyoto was 2012. Smaller event." Concern now in her tone. "Are you alright?"

He hung up without answering. Evelyn wasn't wrong. Evelyn was *never* wrong.

The mug in his hand matched her memory, not his. And he was suddenly very, very alone.

The glyph still pulsed.

It wasn't him that was shifting. It was the world.

By midday his desk was buried in evidence — photos, notes, screenshots. The oak tree. The Chomsky book. The holiday café. The mug. Every anomaly logged in a file he named *Chronos Fade Observations*. A name that tasted like metal in his mouth.

Out the window, the street sign had a new font. The coffee shop's wall now wore a mural in colours so bright it made his eyes ache. The news site mentioned a councillor's scandal he'd never heard of — except, oddly, it rang with that shadow-familiar feeling, like something you'd dreamed but couldn't prove. Arguments flared in the flats nearby, voices thick with confusion.

Then his eyes caught a photo on the mantel — him and his mother, but in front of a house that wasn't theirs. Larger, grander, with stone walls instead of peeling paint. She smiled exactly as she always had.

His thumb brushed her face in the frame. He thought of her forgetting his name, her mind slipping away, the way he'd poured himself into the glyphs for a cure. But if the Fade was rewriting... what if his mother's story — his own life — was nothing more than the current draft of reality?

And the car accident. The tyres, the thud, Sarah's name caught in his throat. Could that vanish too?

The thought chilled him in a way no ghost could. If the past could be rewritten, then there was no past. No him.

Just the Fade. And it was already eating.

Chapter 3: Shared Discrepancies

By midmorning, Alistair's apartment didn't feel like home anymore. It felt like a war room. Every object had become evidence. Every book, photo, newspaper clipping — inspected, compared, logged. His notebooks were filling fast, his handwriting getting smaller and tighter, sometimes slipping into a near-illegible scrawl when his hand started trembling. He hated that tremor. It made the letters stutter, the lines crooked.

He sketched too — little "before" versions of street corners, buildings, facades, from memory. But the moment the pencil left the paper, he knew they were already out of date. Like trying to map a river while it's flooding.

Pacing helped, sort of. He'd worn a shallow oval into the carpet between his desk and the bookshelf. Muffled arguments seeped in from the neighbouring flats — not full-blown shouting, just tense voices carrying words he couldn't quite make out. A low hum of confusion, like the city itself was starting to fray.

Yesterday's oddities — a tree, a book, a mug — had been easy enough to dismiss, in theory. Today, they multiplied.

He went outside, thinking the air would clear him. It didn't.

The oak on the corner now had a small birdhouse tucked into its branches. Painted wood, carved detailing. He stopped dead. That wasn't there. He knew it.

At the café, the smell of beans still hit him like always, but the wall — the bare brick wall that used to be scribbled over with graffiti — now blazed with a mural: galaxies spinning out of impossible geometry. He ordered his usual black, extra strong, as if caffeine could pin his thoughts in place.

The barista — bright blue hair, someone he'd exchanged a thousand casual words with — slid the coffee across the counter. That's when he saw the tattoo. Tiny compass rose, inked into the skin of her wrist.

He glanced at it. She noticed.

"Oh, this?" She smiled, warm and casual. "Got it last year. Keeps me grounded."

Last year. He came in nearly every day. There was no way he'd missed it.

He felt cold, like the heat had been pulled out of his body in one go.

He tried a test on a fellow regular — a retired lit professor with a mind like a steel trap. "That mural," Alistair said, keeping his tone flat, "that's new, right?"

The professor frowned, puzzled by the question. "New? No, no. Been here at least a year. Young artist from the college. Lovely work." His certainty was absolute.

That was worse than if he'd argued. There was no doubt in the man's voice, no pause where the mind tries to reach for something missing. It was gone for him. Completely replaced.

Alistair's stomach turned. He was the outlier now. The glitch. Everyone else was already... updated.

Lena Petrova came to mind. Cognitive psychologist. Memory, collective consciousness, all that. He'd argued with her once — she'd claimed "truth" was just whatever memory the majority agreed on. He'd laughed it off. Now it didn't seem funny.

He found her in his contact list — still there, though he checked twice, half-expecting the name to vanish. Phone call felt too exposed. Email gave him room to control the facts.

No glyphs. No talk of "activation." Just side-by-side photos of the Chomsky book, the mugs, the tree sketches. A clipped, clinical note about discrepancies.

Her reply came fast.

Alistair,
Fascinating. And disturbing. The photos... unsettling. I've seen smaller cases in my patient data — mild collective false memories — nothing on this scale. Your Chomsky example is troubling. Mine's blue too. Or... I thought it was. For a second, I saw something else. This isn't a prank, is it?
My office. 2 PM. Don't be late.

Signed: Lena.

He sat back, staring at the screen. For the first time in days, the pressure in his chest eased — not much, but enough to let him breathe deeper. Someone else saw it. Someone else had felt it shift.

But her last line snagged in his brain: *For a second, I saw something else.*

That “flicker” was how it worked. Sliding into the mind so gently you didn’t notice the rewrite until it was already wearing your old memories like a mask.

The glyph pulsed faintly from his computer, as if it had heard the whole exchange.

This wasn’t just a pattern. It was a trigger. And it was spreading.

The world wasn’t solid anymore. It was water. And he was one of the last few left treading in it, watching the rest sink without even knowing they were drowning.

Chapter 4: The Historical Erosion

The morning after the fabricated self, Alistair woke with a heaviness that wasn't just fatigue. This one lived in his bones. It pressed at the back of his eyes. Even breathing felt... deliberate.

The hum hadn't left. That low, constant frequency, somewhere under hearing but inside his head all the same. It was patient. Persuasive. *Let go.*

He hadn't slept properly. The faces kept cycling — Clara's quick smile, the Tuscan light on oil paint, the sharp, dry wind of the Sahara dig. Some of them belonged to him. Some didn't. They all felt equally real, which was the worst part. His mind had become a palimpsest — layers over layers, scraped and rewritten, but the ghost lines still showing through.

He realised, too late, that he was sketching. Hand loose, moving easily, producing a sun-washed villa he'd never seen. Olive trees, too exact to be imagined. The comfort of its geometry was almost pleasant — almost — before he shoved the pad away and rubbed at his temples.

Coffee. That was something he knew. Coffee was an anchor.
Except today the steps felt like he was miming them. Filter slips. The scoop lands off-centre. Grounds spill like black sand over the counter. The smell rose sharp

and bitter but somehow muted, like smelling it through glass.

The city outside was worse. A glass tower slicing the sky where the brutalist government block had been since forever. The park's path bent differently, trees all wrong — young, too green, too tidy. He walked through like a ghost, weaving between bodies that didn't see him, all of them wearing the same serene acceptance of a world he didn't recognise.

Lena looked older. Not aged — drained. Movements slow, eyes rimmed dark. A small teddy bear in her grip, fur matted from years of use.

"Lily's favourite," she said, and her voice had no edge, no clinical cadence. "It's getting worse, Alistair. The dreams. The... touches. I wake up reaching for her. I hear her laugh." She pressed her fingers into the bear until her knuckles whitened. "It's so tempting. Like sinking into a warm blanket."

He knew. He didn't say he knew, but he did. "The Fade's not just changing the past," he told her. "It's rewriting how we feel now. Making the fake ones warmer. More vivid than what's real."

He told her about the library. The shifting affiliations. The archaeological 'discovery.' "It's trying to wear us down. Offer a better version. One we'll stop fighting." His palm scraped over stubble, the rasp loud in the quiet office. "Haven't shaved in days. Stupid thing to notice. But that's another bit of me... sliding."

Her smile was thin, brittle. "Trivialities are anchors, Alistair. And they're being cut." She flicked a hand toward her screen. "It's not just us. It's growing. I've got a case — boy, seven years old. Severe night terrors. Calls it 'The Great Scourge.'"

Alistair felt the muscles in his jaw tighten. "A war?"

Her fingers stumbled on the keyboard — rare for her. "Sky-fire. Metal beasts. Hiding in bunkers. Burning cities. He lists battles. Names commanders. Uniforms. He says he was there. Cries for friends lost in the trenches." Her voice, which started clinical, caught and thinned.

"A war that never happened?"

"Not in our timeline," she whispered. "But for him, the trauma's... pure. I work with memory. With perception. And this—" Her hands curled into fists, trembling on the desk. "It defies everything I've studied. I tried to explain it — delusion, mass hallucination — but it's too sharp. Too consistent. I cross-referenced. Found traces in old papers. Gone now."

She jabbed a finger at the transcript. It shook. "He named 'General Kael.' Search turned up nothing. Then, for one second, a 1987 news piece — praising his strategy. And gone."

The chair's legs scraped hard as she pushed back. The sound was ugly in the quiet. She buried her face in her hands. Shoulders shook. "What do I tell his parents? My whole career's been about understanding the mind. Healing it. But if the truth keeps shifting, if there's no fixed point..." Her words were muffled now, breaking. "...then I can't fix anything. My patients. My work. All of it... meaningless. I'm failing them. Failing everyone."

Alistair felt it in his gut — the kind of terror that went beyond personal dread. This wasn't a misprinted date or a green book cover. This was the construction of a war that took millions, in a history now dissolving. And Lena — brilliant, stubborn Lena — was fracturing.

He reached across the desk. Hovered for a moment, then laid his hand over hers. Cold skin. Damp. She didn't pull away.

"This isn't just individual memory," he said. "It's rewriting collective trauma. Building whole histories — complete with their dead — and then trying to wipe them clean." His mother flashed into his mind. The way her eyes had emptied. This was the same disease, scaled up to civilisation.

Lena's gaze was fixed on the boy's transcript. A tear slipped down her cheek. "If it can make a war, what else? What else is it planting in us?"

He knew. The glyphs. Not just keys to memory. Blueprints. The machinery for reality.

It wasn't random. It had intent.

And then — soft as breath — something touched his mind. A push. A suggestion: *Stop questioning*.

He flinched, tightened his grip on her hand.

A promise. Unspoken.

They would fight.

Chapter 5: Identity in Flux

The revelation of *The Great Scourge* left him unsteady, like he'd taken a blow he hadn't seen coming. A war that had never existed in his own memory, yet had carved trauma into a child in Lena's care. He'd thought he understood the Fade. Thought it was rearranging, pruning. But this—this was composition. Full symphonies. New histories, complete with their discord, their casualties.

And under it, that damned hum again. The promise. Clara's laugh. Clara's touch. A quiet, perfect life if he just... let go. It came at him like a counter-melody, wrapping around the noise of these fabricated wars. For one reckless second, he wanted it. Wanted the simplicity of one lie that didn't splinter, didn't keep changing.

The warmth started then. Slow. Gentle. Spreading through his chest like sunlight through a curtain. And he knew it wasn't his. The Fade's touch. A reward for thinking the right thoughts. He flinched, jaw tightening. Ran his tongue over his teeth — nervous habit, but today it felt like more. Something to tether him.

The days that followed were taut, everything sharp at the edges. Every street corner suspect. Every headline a potential landmine. Even the smallest exchanges could be traps — a nod from a shopkeeper, a laugh from someone passing by. The city didn't hold still. Facades shifted. Parks re-angled their paths. The strangers he passed weren't quite the same from one day to the next.

The air smelled different too. Still the exhaust and warm bread and street dust — but laced now with something faint, clinical. Like ozone after a storm you can't quite remember. Somewhere in the distance, voices tangled in arguments over details of history. Quiet but constant. Like the sound of a beehive pressed to your ear.

Lena was slipping deeper into her ghost-child's gravity. The teddy bear never left her hand anymore. Even mid-discussion, even when her tone sharpened, she'd stroke the fur absently. And she spoke of Lily the way people speak of their dead — full of small, physical details.

"I found a lock of hair this morning," she whispered, holding out a thread of blonde so fine it was almost invisible. Her voice caught. "It was in a locket. I don't remember owning the locket. But it's hers, Alistair. I know it."

The look in her eyes — not hysteria, not doubt. Certainty. And relief, as though the Fade had given her back something precious. It chilled him more than her grief. *What if this was how it won?* By making the resistance sweeter to surrender.

"It's so hard to fight it," she said, barely audible. "When it gives you something so... real. So warm."

He inhaled sharply, forcing the air all the way down, dragging himself back into the room. Mutters under his breath — an old habit, born of too many hours without someone else to listen.

But the Fade wasn't content to work through other people anymore.

One morning, he woke as if pulled up from a deep dive, lungs burning. The dream clung. Not a linguist. A painter. A life in a sunlit Tuscan studio, walls lined with canvases, turpentine thick in the air. The weight of the brush in his hand, colours blooming under his touch, the quiet satisfaction of trapping light on canvas. It wasn't a memory — and yet it was.

He shook it off. Glasses on the bedside table, the ritual a kind of defiance.

Later, rummaging through his office for a journal, he opened a drawer he almost never touched. There it was. A small leather-bound sketchbook.

He didn't own a sketchbook. He wasn't an artist.

But it sat solid in his hand, the leather worn where a thumb had rested over and over.

Inside: charcoal landscapes, portraits, still lifes. Confident lines. Skilled shading. And then—

A self-portrait. Younger. Same eyes but with something different in them — a looseness, a quiet danger. The jaw softer. Hair a little longer. On the page opposite: *June 2008* in his handwriting, and one word in looping script. *Crepuscolo*.

He stared at the page. No memory of drawing it. No memory of being that man. And yet—his lines, his script. A cold weight sank in his gut. Was this a life forgotten, or a life still being glued into place?

The accident tugged at the edge of his mind, slippery, shifting. Had that been rewritten too?

The sketchbook hummed faintly in his hands. Not imagined. A vibration. A confirmation. The ache bloomed suddenly in his wrist — as though he'd spent hours with a brush pinched between his fingers.

Lena was unraveling on her own timeline.

His phone rang in the evening. Her voice on the other end — thin, shaking. "Alistair... I just got home. My apartment... it's different. The layout. The furniture. Not mine. But it *feels* like mine. And there's a child's drawing on the fridge. A cat. A terrible cat. But—" her breath hitched "—it's hers. I... I don't have a child. Do I?"

He was at her door within the hour.

Inside — warmer colours, the edges of things softened. A small bedroom painted in bright pastels, stuffed animals lined along the wall. The fridge held the cat drawing — all crayon squiggles and a crooked smile.

Lena stood in the living room, pale, trembling, her eyes caught between him and the fridge.

"Her name is Lily," she whispered. "I know it. I remember her laugh, the way she clung to my leg, her lullaby, the smell of her hair after a bath. But there's nothing. No photos. No papers. No pregnancy. Just—" her voice broke "—just the memories." Tears slid unchecked. "I remember a life where I was a researcher, obsessed with work. And I remember a life where I was a mother. A mother who's just lost her child. Which one's the lie, Alistair? Which one's the truth? I can't— I can't take this."

The drawing on the fridge seemed to give off a faint warmth. He could almost see it seeping into her, shoring up the false memory until it was unshakable.

Something in his chest twisted. This wasn't about altered headlines or book covers. This was identity theft at the most intimate level. Fabricating grief, embedding it so deep the body wept for it.

He stepped forward, pulled her into his arms. She clung back, her sobs shaking them both.

Two people adrift in a current they couldn't stop, holding onto the only thing left that felt real — each other.

Chapter 6: The Unwritten Diary

The shared grief over Lena's phantom child bound them in a way nothing else could have. Not friendship. Not work. Something sharper, more desperate. Lily — a little girl who, by every rational measure, had never existed — now existed completely in Lena's memory. And in her grief.

It wasn't a grief with a past. No timeline to point to. Just... there. Present. Heavy. A sorrow born from a now that made no sense.

Alistair could feel it pressing on him too — not the child, but the truth it pointed to. The Fade wasn't just repainting the world. It was rewiring the ability to connect. To share history. To love. And if it could give her a daughter and the hollow ache of losing her... what could it give him? What could it take away?

That's when he felt it — a faint pressure in his head, so slight it could've been the ghost of a thought. Like a hand, resting just behind the mind, nudging him. *Maybe it's not horror,* the touch suggested. *Maybe it's kindness. A gift.*

He jerked away from the idea. Physically, as though there were something to shake off. His hand found a pen, twisted the cap, closed it again. Twist. Close. Twist. Close. The small, repetitive click grounding him in the absurdity of the moment.

Their meetings became more frantic, less about catching up and more about trading warnings. The anomalies came faster. Bigger.

One week, an international treaty they both remembered as signed and celebrated... was now a failure that had led to ten years of political strain neither had lived through. Paintings they knew — studied — now had new brushstrokes, altered shades, figures shifted by a hand centuries dead.

Even the city was warping in plain sight. At the edge of his vision, buildings swayed into new shapes. A bridge he'd crossed a hundred times now carried an ornate extra arch — weathered stone that looked as though it had been there for a century.

"It's like a dream," he muttered one afternoon, staring through Lena's window at the barely familiar skyline. He rubbed his temples. The ache there felt old. "A lucid dream, except the dreamer's someone else. And we're just... characters. Badly written ones." The smile he tried to give her crumbled before it reached his eyes.

Lena didn't look up from her patient files. "Worse than a dream. Dreams end. This doesn't. This resists." Her hand moved through her hair, snagging on a tangle. She tapped a folder. "History professor. Fought with his family about an event he remembered the 'old' way. Next day — aphasia. Couldn't remember any history. Not the old version. Not the new."

Alistair's stomach tightened. The Fade wasn't passive. It punished. It defended itself.

Something brushed his thoughts then, quiet, persuasive: *Stop resisting. Let go.*

He pushed back — hard. Pulled in a deep breath, tried to anchor himself to the present. And muttered under his breath, the way he always did when there was no one left to answer.

By late afternoon, he couldn't take any more theory or dread. He walked to the little coffee shop on the corner. Independent. Always smelled like toasted beans and cinnamon. He ordered his usual — black, extra strong — and took the seat by the window. Watched people go by. Faces calm. Steps unhurried.

For a few minutes, he envied them.

Then the shouting started.

Across the street, outside the local historical society, an old man was bellowing at a young volunteer. His face flushed, eyes wide, jabbing at a newly mounted plaque.

"It was the Great Fire of '76!" he roared. "Not the Urban Renewal Project! My grandfather's shop burned to the ground! I *smelled* the smoke!"

The woman flinched at his volume but tried to soothe him. "Sir, the records— they say it was a planned renewal. There's no record of a fire like that. Maybe your memory—"

"Tricks?!" he barked, and the word came out like an insult. His grip clamped around her arm. "I was there! My family lost everything!"

A few heads turned. Discomfort passed through the crowd like a quick shiver, and then... avoidance. The couple holding hands glanced once and walked faster. A man on his phone shook his head and looked away, the way you do at someone muttering on the bus.

No one challenged him. No one seemed curious. They'd already absorbed the new truth.

Alistair watched with a cold weight in his gut. This was the same thing as the professor's aphasia — but raw, public. A lone voice shouting into a void where no one else remembered what he remembered.

Again, the push came. Soft, tempting: *You don't need to carry this.*

He gripped the coffee cup, the bitterness sharp and grounding on his tongue. Forced a breath. Forced himself back into the room.

That night, his apartment felt smaller, the quiet denser. The glyph on his computer pulsed faintly. Watching.

He was cataloguing the latest alterations when his eyes caught on something under a stack of papers — a leather-bound journal. Plain cover. Not his. He didn't keep a diary.

He opened it. Blank pages first, then his handwriting. Tight, precise, unmistakable.

October 17th, [unknown year]: The rain today was relentless, mirroring the ache in my chest. She's gone. It's been three weeks. The silence is a physical weight. I keep expecting her in the study. The doctors say it was sudden, unexpected. But I know. It was the loneliness that took her. My beautiful Clara.

He froze.

Clara? No. His wife — the woman he loved — was Sarah. Sarah, killed in the screech and shatter of a car crash. Sarah, who quoted old poetry and argued with him about syntax.

He flipped faster now. More entries. A shared cottage by the sea. A garden. A quiet life. Evenings together. He, a philosophy lecturer, not a linguist. The grief on the page was thick and detailed, and the longer he read, the more he could feel it in his own chest.

The warmth in his palms started slow. The words settling in as if they belonged there. Sarah's image flickered.

He slammed the book shut. His mind reeled.

The accident. The glass. Sarah's still body. Was that the truth? Or was it already another fabrication, swapped in for something else years ago?

He stumbled to his computer. Typed *Clara Finch*. Nothing. Typed *Alistair Finch philosopher*. A handful of irrelevant hits. *Sarah Finch car accident*. No confirmation. No proof. The internet had been bent too.

He looked at the diary again. Then the photo of his mother on his desk — except now she stood in front of a house he didn't recognise. Bigger. Older.

Was that *Clara's* house?

His skin prickled. This wasn't about history anymore. It was about identity. His. Lena's. The Fade could graft lives onto them like new limbs. And he could already feel the phantom ache of losing someone who'd never been real.

He closed his eyes. Pressed his palms against them until stars burst in the dark.

When he opened them again, his gaze landed on the glyph diagrams in his notes. And he saw it.

A pattern he'd written off years ago. Not a word. Not even language as humans understood it. But the rhythm of it, the frequency — it meant something.

To cleanse. To prepare. For the next cycle.

His throat went dry. It wasn't random. It wasn't chaotic.

It was a process. Ancient. And deliberate.

Chapter 7: The Collective Amnesia

The diary sat on his desk like it had always been there. Not a file, not a scrap of research — but a whole other life bound in leather. A life with Clara. Quiet mornings. Evenings by the fire. Philosophy instead of linguistics. He stared at it. At his own hands. At the dark window where his reflection hovered back — pale, uncertain, split.

Which one was he? Alistair Finch, the failed linguist who'd watched Sarah die in a mess of glass and screaming brakes? Or the philosopher who'd held Clara's hand as she slipped away in the quiet of their seaside cottage?

Both lives felt solid. Both griefs sat heavy and sharp, each one certain in its own way. Sarah's accident flickered at the edge of his mind like a bad signal. Had that been rewritten too?

The guilt that had driven him for years... maybe it wasn't his at all. Maybe it had been planted — something for him to cling to so he wouldn't notice the rest of the truth eroding.

The diary gave a faint tremor, or maybe he imagined it. Not a sound — more like a pulse through the wood of the desk. And with it, the softest pull, the gentlest nudge toward accepting Clara as real.

He was so tired. Not just mind-tired — bone-tired. Even breathing felt like work. His meals had been cups of coffee gone cold beside stacks of notes.

He drew in a sharp breath, forcing his mind to stay here, now. Muttered something under his breath, because there was no one else to listen anymore.

He called Lena. His voice came out rough, words spilling fast, almost tripping over themselves — the diary, the entries, Clara.

She listened. The silence on her end was heavy, broken only by short, sharp questions.

When he finished, she exhaled audibly. "It's not just history anymore," she said, her voice pulled tight, something trembling under it. "It's an ontological rewrite. Full personal histories. Emotions to match. My Lily. Your Clara. It's building identities from scratch. We're just... puppets." She tried to laugh at her own metaphor, but it died between them.

They met at the public library — neutral ground, the smell of paper and floor polish. But even here, the Fade had been. The statue in the entrance hall was wrong now — new man, new name, new deeds carved in bronze.

Nobody else noticed. Students hunched over tables, arguing details of a history Alistair had never heard, certain and unshakable. He felt the ache of it — their calm assurance, their untouched conviction.

"The resistance is futile," Lena said quietly, watching them. "My professor's aphasia... it's worse. He can't speak properly now. I told his family I couldn't help him." Her hand dragged through her hair, slow and heavy. "I've never felt so useless."

Alistair's stomach knotted. The Fade was watching. Reacting. Punishing.

The soft push came again: *Let go.*

He fought it. "We can't give up," he said, low but fierce, gripping her arm for a second longer than necessary. She looked exhausted. Her hands trembled.

He decided to push back harder.

That afternoon's faculty meeting was perfect. The room was airless, fluorescent. Professor Harrison droned about budget cuts. Alistair waited, then dropped it in casually: "Over fifty years since the moon landing, eh? July 20th, 1969. United the whole planet for a moment."

He remembered it in perfect detail — seven years old, knees itchy from the rug, his mother's arm around him as Armstrong stepped onto the moon. Her whisper: *Remember this, Alistair. This is history.*

Harrison frowned. "July 20th? Everyone knows it was September 12th. Autumn equinox. New beginnings." He chuckled. Others nodded.

September 12th. Wrong. Utterly wrong.

Alistair pressed. "No, it was summer. I remember—"

Davies cut in gently. "You're mixing it with an earlier Apollo mission. The real landing was September. My dad watched it."

Their certainty was absolute. No hesitation. The Fade had overwritten them cleanly.

Something warm bloomed in his chest — not comfort exactly, but the shape of it. Urging him to accept.

He refused.

Back in his office, he wrote it all down — new date, altered timelines, invented "weather window." The isolation closed in. He didn't recognise the man in the window's reflection.

That night, he almost slept — until the whisper started. Not words at first, just the low hum of a thousand forgotten things. Then, clear as a voice in the room: *Why resist? This is the new truth. Forget.*

He shot upright, breath tearing through him. The thought wasn't his.

The diary. The phantom wife. It wasn't random. It was a strategy — give him a new past, make it easier to erase the old.

He dragged a hand through his hair. "Damn it," he told the empty room. "I don't want to forget her. I don't want to forget Sarah."

The words hung there, raw and bare, with nothing neat to follow them.

Chapter 8: The Shifting Sands of Self

The whisper didn't stop after he woke. It stayed in his head like a low note on a broken instrument, vibrating in the marrow. Not words, exactly — more like the idea of them. Forget. Rest. Let go.

It promised the obvious things: no more static in the brain, no more tearing at the seams of memory. It promised Clara. The cottage. A guiltless life where Sarah never died in the road with her hair across her face.

The temptation wasn't dramatic. It was slow, warm. Like slipping into a bath that's a little too hot but feels better the longer you're in. He fought it anyway, clinging to the sharp-edged bits of himself that still belonged to him. It felt ridiculous — like a drowning man clutching splinters while the tide tried to coax him under.

He could almost feel the Fade there with him. Cold air against his neck. Watching. Not moving in for the kill yet — just leaning on him, a constant hand in the small of his back, guiding him toward the easier version of things.

His hair was damp at the temples from sweat. He dragged a hand through it and let the groan come out without censoring it. He hadn't slept more than two or three hours at a stretch in days. The weight of it was physical now, pressing down on his shoulders, making him clumsy.

The apartment had stopped being his safe place. It was just another front in whatever this was. Every photograph, every mug, every familiar object was suspect. He found himself staring at old pictures until his eyes ached, searching for the joins between what was and what had been put there.

One photo — him and his father, fishing. It used to be a mountain stream, biting cold on the ankles, smell of pine sap in the air. Now it was a sleek fiberglass boat on a wide, sun-washed lake. The emotional part was unchanged — the weight of his father's hand on his shoulder, the quiet patience. But the image... wrong. It even shimmered once, just a little flicker over the surface, like it was mocking him for thinking he'd caught it out.

He tried to make tea. Simple. Automatic. But his hands shook so badly he almost poured boiling water over them.

Lena was coming apart too. The teddy bear was with her all the time now, its fur matted, one glass eye dulled. "Lily" wasn't just in her head anymore. She was in the room. Lena could feel her. Tiny fingers in her palm. The faint, powdery sweetness of baby lotion. Sometimes a giggle from the hallway that stopped her mid-sentence.

Then the "proof" started turning up. A child's sock, rolled and tucked behind a sofa cushion. A crayon sun folded between the pages of a book. A milk tooth in a small box. Each one a cut — and each one proving nothing at all, because the girl didn't exist.

“It’s not just wiping us clean, Alistair,” Lena said the next time they met. Her voice was tighter than usual, but shaking underneath. Eyes rimmed red. “It’s... replacing us. With so much detail, so much beauty, that the old self just can’t compete.”

She swallowed. Looked at him. “What if the ‘old’ reality is the fake? What if this is the truth, and we’re clinging to our own lie?” Her hands shook where they rested in her lap. “God, sometimes I want to let it happen. Just... be done.”

Something in him went cold at that. Because it wasn’t only her speaking — it was the Fade, wearing her voice. Using her empathy like a lure.

On his desk at home, the glyph pulsed faintly. Not just light, but a kind of *tone*, deep enough to feel in the teeth. The whispers in his head shifted from suggestion to full narrative — whole biographies sliding into place. Him as a crofter’s son on the moors. Him as a painter in Brazil. As an architect named Eleanor’s husband. As a diplomat with Marcus at his side. Each one rich, consistent, emotionally airtight.

He opened the “Chronos Fade Observations” file. The moon landing entry was still there — July 20th, 1969. He fixed his eyes on it, willing it to hold.

Look away. Look back. Flicker.
August 5th, 1971.
Then — snap — September 12th, 1969.

His mouth filled with the metallic taste of a dying battery. Static on the tongue. The Fade wasn’t just editing the world now. It was editing him.

Outside his little orbit, reality kept shedding skin. Politicians gave speeches at noon, and by night the transcripts said something different — whole positions reversed. TV anchors denied ever having reported what they had, on tape, twelve hours before. People stopped talking about the past altogether. It was safer.

He tried one more time to show proof. Brought two Chomsky books, two mugs, a series of photographs into the common room. Laid them out in front of Harrison.

Harrison looked at them with a sort of patient pity. "They're both green, Alistair. Always have been."

"No, this one's blue," Alistair said, holding it up, voice pitching higher. "Look. Feel the paper, the lettering—"

Harrison shook his head slowly. The green cover in his hands seemed to hum, as if pleased with itself.

And the room was watching now, a few heads turned just enough to signal concern without commitment.

By the time he got home, the exhaustion had teeth. That night the whispers came back, full chorus. Clara was there this time. Her hand on his arm in the kitchen. The studio light in Tuscany. The sound of the sea through an open window. All of it precise. All of it safe.

He shoved his palms into his eyes until stars popped behind them. "Sarah," he whispered. "I don't want to lose you."

It felt, more than anything, like he was talking to himself.

Chapter 9: The Fabricated Self

The Fade's pull wasn't quiet anymore. It didn't lurk in the corners of thought — it sat in the middle of his mind, constant, steady. A hum you couldn't turn off. Not even a song, exactly. More like something the body heard before the brain caught up.

Clara. Tuscany. A kitchen with no ghosts in it. A version of himself that had never held Sarah's cold hand in the road. They weren't just flickers now — they came in full colour, with the smell of baking bread and the warm ache of sun on his neck.

He dug his nails into his palms until he felt skin break. The sting was an anchor. Small. Stupid. But his.

A dull ache sat behind his eyes like a weight. He kept checking his phone for Lena's name — ridiculous, compulsive. Just to know someone else was still in this with him.

He muttered to himself without meaning to, words tumbling out like they needed air. Nobody to hear them anyway.

Outside, the world kept shifting. It wasn't just books or dates now. Whole buildings gone overnight, replaced by shapes and styles that felt... imported from somewhere else. But they were built into the city like they'd always been here. People passed them without so much as a pause. No one noticed. No one remembered.

He caught pieces of arguments drifting from café tables — voices getting heated over some "historical" event that clearly had changed since breakfast. No one seemed surprised for long. The dissonance settled into a low-grade hum of acceptance.

Lena wasn't holding on well. The teddy bear had appeared three days ago and now she carried it everywhere, tucked against her side like a secret. She said it was Lily's favourite.

Her eyes looked different now. Less sharp, more... blurred at the edges. Like the light had gone slightly wrong in them.

"I found myself humming a lullaby this morning," she told him at their next meeting, her voice almost gone. "One I've never heard before. I knew the words."

Her lips trembled. Tears slid down, slow.

"It was Lily's. I'm losing myself, Alistair. I'm becoming her. The mother who lost a child. And I don't know which one of me is the lie anymore. I just want it to stop."

Her face fell into her hands. Shoulders shaking. No sound but the air between them.

He felt it — that cold rush in the spine. She was going. The Fade wasn't erasing her; it was moving in, wearing her like skin.

He touched her arm, light. "We'll find a way," he said, voice breaking on the promise.

Back in his apartment, he decided to push. To see if there was anything they couldn't take from him. His work, maybe. The part of himself built from decades of lectures, papers, stubborn fights in conference halls.

The university library smelled the same — paper, varnish, dust. But it felt different. Like stepping into a place that had already decided you didn't belong.

He went straight to the shelves. Fingers over the spines. Found it. *The Syntactic Paradox: A New Approach to Pre-Human Communication.*

The cover was right. The logo right. His name on the title page... mostly right. But underneath: *Professor of Comparative Philosophy, University of Edinburgh.*

Edinburgh. Philosophy.

He'd never taught there. Never studied it seriously.

The acknowledgements listed strangers. Thanked them for "metaphysical debates." The dedication stopped his breath. *To Clara, my truest muse, whose quiet wisdom illuminated every page.*

The book slid out of his hands and hit the carpet with a dull sound.

This wasn't a dream-life anymore. It was etched into his record. He wasn't a linguist who'd been rewritten. He was — in this version — a philosopher. The other life was the ghost now.

His skull throbbed, deep and rhythmic.

He walked out fast, the world outside spinning in tiny, disorienting ways. A newsstand caught his eye — headlines about a lost civilization in the Sahara. Monumental ruins. An untranslatable language.

He had never heard of it. Yet the photos looked like they'd been in textbooks for years.

And then — the inset image. Him. Younger, dust-streaked, grinning like he'd just won a war. Holding a carved fragment up to the sun.

The Fade wasn't satisfied with swapping out the past. It was giving him *too many*. The painter. The philosopher. The archaeologist. All convincing. All rich with moments he could almost remember living.

He wanted to sit down. Right there on the pavement. Shut his eyes and let them close over him.

The chorus in his head got louder. Not suggestion now — instruction. *Let go. Pick one. Stop clawing at the edges.*

Clara's laugh. Lily's hand in his. Sunlight over Tuscan hills.

Back in the apartment, the glyph on the screen pulsed like a heartbeat, warm and wrong. It wasn't inviting anymore. It was pulling.

And God help him — he wanted to go.

He sank into the sofa. Face in his hands. "This is too much," he whispered into the dark space between his palms. "I can't... I can't keep track anymore."

Chapter 10: The War That Never Was

The grotesque absurdity of Van Gogh as "the Sun King's Painter" and Beethoven as an exiled Brazilian revolutionary clawed at Alistair's mind, each fabricated detail a fresh wound to his intellectual integrity. These weren't just historical footnotes; they were pillars of human culture, now reshaped by an unseen hand. The Fade wasn't merely editing; it was performing an elaborate, terrifying act of cultural vandalism, replacing the messy, inspiring truths of human struggle with narratives of its own design. The siren song of oblivion, offering the serene life with Clara, intensified, a cruel counterpoint to the growing cacophony of fabricated histories. A part of him, a deeply weary part, yearned for the simplicity of a single, coherent lie, any lie, as long as it promised an end to the agonizing dissonance. As this yearning swelled, a faint, almost imperceptible warmth spread through his chest, a comforting sensation that seemed to emanate from the very air around him, a silent invitation to surrender, to embrace the fabricated peace. He flinched, recognizing the Fade's insidious touch, its direct response to his internal struggle, a malevolent lullaby. He found himself constantly rubbing the bridge of his nose, a new habit, as if trying to physically wipe away the persistent mental fog.

His days became a blur of frantic documentation and escalating dread. He found himself compulsively checking historical archives, scientific journals. And news sites, only to find the "new" reality solidified, reinforced by countless corroborating sources. The digital world, once a bastion of verifiable information, had become the Fade's most efficient tool for propagating its new truths, a vast, seamless tapestry of lies. The city outside his window continued its silent, architectural ballet, buildings appearing and disappearing, their new forms seamlessly integrated into the urban tapestry. He saw a familiar bookstore now replaced by a bustling tech startup, its glass facade reflecting a sky that felt a shade too bright, too artificial. He knew the bookstore had been there for thirty years, its dusty shelves a comfort. Now, it was gone. And no one else seemed to remember it, their faces blank with acceptance. He even caught himself humming a tune he didn't recognize, a cheerful, upbeat melody that felt entirely alien to his current state of mind, yet somehow comforting, a subtle intrusion from the Fade.

Lena, meanwhile, was sinking deeper into her phantom grief. The aftermath of her public breakdown at the peer review session had left her even more fragile. She'd been granted a "mandatory leave of absence," a polite dismissal that felt like a professional death sentence. Lily's teddy bear was never far from her grasp, clutched almost protectively, a talisman against a grief that was both real and fabricated. Sometimes Alistair would find her humming the unfamiliar lullaby, a faraway, almost blissful look in her eyes. The emotional resonance of her fabricated child was so profound that it often eclipsed the horror of their shared predicament, pulling her into a terrifying, yet comforting, delusion. "I dreamt of her last night, Alistair," she confided, her voice soft, almost ethereal, her eyes glazed with unshed tears. "She was laughing. And I felt... happy. Truly happy. It was so real. Sometimes, I wish I could just stay there, in that dream, with her. It's so much easier than this." Her words were a chilling echo of Alistair's own temptation, a testament to the Fade's insidious power to offer solace in its lies. He knew the Fade was using this emotional bond, this manufactured love, to neutralize her resistance, to make her a willing participant in her own erasure, a mother lost in a dream of her child, forever cradling a phantom grief, her intellect slowly subsumed by manufactured affection, her very essence softening into a malleable, forgetful bliss.

The historical erosion now began to target figures of cultural significance, the very titans of human creativity. Alistair, seeking a moment of respite, a fleeting connection to a stable past, had turned on the classical music station, a familiar comfort, a balm for his frayed nerves. A piece by Ludwig van Beethoven began to play – his Fifth Symphony, a monumental work he knew note for note, its opening chords a defiant cry against fate. But as the familiar, thunderous opening swelled, the announcer's voice broke in, smooth and unctuous.

"That was the magnificent 'Symphony of Resolve' by Ludwig van Beethoven, composed, as many of you know, during his arduous exile in the Americas, a period of profound personal struggle and artistic triumph against the oppressive colonial regime."

Alistair froze, his hand hovering over the radio dial, his blood running cold. Exile in the Americas? Beethoven had never left Europe. He was a German composer, renowned for his life in Vienna, a man who battled his own body, his increasing deafness, to create works of unparalleled genius. The Fifth Symphony was composed during a period of increasing deafness, a battle against physical infirmity, a defiant roar against personal tragedy, not geopolitical banishment. The very essence of the man, his struggle, his triumph, was being rewritten. He felt a sudden, sharp pain in his chest, a purely psychosomatic ache, as if a part of his own history, his own understanding of human greatness, had just been ripped away.

He scrambled to his computer, his fingers flying across the keyboard, a desperate need for verification overriding his growing dread. He searched for "Beethoven biography." The results were immediate, unanimous. Ludwig van Beethoven, born in Bonn, Germany, had indeed spent a significant portion of his creative life in the Americas, specifically in a small, isolated colony in what was now modern-day Brazil. His "Symphony of Resolve" was directly inspired by his struggles against the oppressive colonial regime, a defiant anthem of freedom for the downtrodden. His deafness, the articles now stated, was a minor, late-life affliction, a mere inconvenience, not the defining tragedy Alistair remembered, not the crucible that forged his greatest works. The internet, the supposed bastion of immutable information, had become the Fade's most efficient tool for propagating its new truths, a vast, seamless tapestry of lies.

Alistair felt a profound sense of violation, a deep, personal loss that went beyond mere facts. Beethoven, the defiant genius battling his own body, the titan of classical music whose struggle had always resonated deeply with Alistair's own intellectual battles, his own fight against the creeping oblivion of Sarah's memory, was gone. Replaced by a different figure, a different narrative, a different source of inspiration. It was as if a beloved friend had been rewritten, their core essence altered beyond recognition, their very soul re-sculpted. This wasn't just a historical shift; it was an emotional amputation, a cultural lobotomy. As he stared at the screen, a faint, almost imperceptible hum resonated from his computer speakers, a low, soothing frequency that seemed to affirm the new biography, subtly reinforcing its "correctness" in his mind. He slammed his fist on the desk, a frustrated growl escaping him. "No! This isn't right! This isn't him!"

He called Lena, his voice tight with a new kind of despair, a raw edge of desperation. "It's Beethoven, Lena. They've changed Beethoven. His entire life story. His exile. His inspiration. It's... it's a mockery. It's like they're trying to erase everything that made him great, everything that made him human."

Lena was silent for a moment, a heavy pause that spoke volumes. "I just read a news article about a new exhibition on Vincent van Gogh," she finally said, her voice strained, a tremor running through it, but with a new, chilling note of detached observation. "They're showcasing a series of his 'lost' works, vibrant, joyful landscapes painted during his years as a court artist for the Dutch monarchy. They're calling him 'the Sun King's Painter'. Imagine. Van Gogh. A court painter." She let out a short, bitter laugh, devoid of humor. "It's almost funny, isn't it?.. The tortured artist, now a gilded cage pet. What's next, Shakespeare writing sonnets for corporate sponsors?.." For a fleeting moment, Alistair noticed how tired she looked, the shadows under her eyes deeper than before, her hands trembling slightly as if holding back more than words.

Alistair felt a cold, hollow dread, deeper than any he'd known. Van Gogh, the tortured, brilliant artist who cut off his ear, who painted with a furious, desperate energy born of mental anguish and poverty, whose canvases screamed with the raw, beautiful agony of his soul, now a court painter? The absurdity was grotesque, a mockery of artistic suffering, a systematic dismantling of the very concept of artistic genius born of struggle.

"It's targeting the very foundations of our culture, Alistair," Lena continued, her voice gaining a chilling edge of detached observation, as if she were a scientist analyzing her own impending doom. "The narratives we tell ourselves. The heroes we admire. The struggles that define us. If it can rewrite Beethoven and Van Gogh, what's next?.. Shakespeare?.. Newton?.. The very concepts of genius and inspiration?.. The very meaning of human endeavor?.. It's like it's trying to streamline humanity, remove all the messy, unpredictable bits."

Alistair felt the walls of his reality closing in, the air growing heavy, suffocating. The Fade wasn't just erasing; it was re-sculpting the collective unconscious, replacing the raw, messy truths of human achievement with sanitized, convenient, or entirely new narratives. And the most terrifying part was the ease with which humanity absorbed these new truths. He saw people discussing Beethoven's "exile" with casual familiarity, as if it had always been part of their knowledge, their faces serene in their ignorance. Their acceptance was the Fade's greatest triumph, a testament to its insidious power. He looked at his computer screen, the glyph pulsing with a faint, almost triumphant glow, its light seeming to expand and contract with a slow, deliberate rhythm, as if it were breathing, watching him, inviting him to finally let go. The whispers in his mind were no longer just offering a new life; they were weaving intricate narratives of his own "new" pasts, complete with the emotional resonance of those lives. He saw himself, the philosopher, debating with "Clara" in a sun-drenched garden, their intellectual connection profound and comforting. He saw himself, the painter, capturing the Brazilian landscape that had inspired the "new" Beethoven, a life of artistic fulfillment, a life of peace. The Fade was not just trying to make him forget; it was trying to make him choose which fabricated reality he would inhabit, offering him a seemingly peaceful escape from the agonizing truth of his own, dying world. And in his profound weariness, the choice felt less like a battle and more like an inevitability, a surrender to the rewritten cosmos. He reached for Lena's hand across the table, a silent plea for shared strength. Her grip was surprisingly firm, a fragile anchor in the chaos. "We can't let it win," he whispered, his voice raw with a desperate resolve. "Not completely."

Chapter 11: The Reimagined Maestro

The grotesque absurdity of it stuck in Alistair's head like a splinter: Van Gogh as *the Sun King's Painter*. Beethoven, not in Vienna, not deaf and raging at fate, but some exiled Brazilian revolutionary. Each lie was like a scalpel cut, clean but deep, slicing away at the bedrock of everything he'd ever trusted. These weren't obscure trivia facts you could shrug off. They were pillars. Keystones. The kind of stories a culture builds itself around.

The Fade wasn't just tweaking details. It was vandalising — deliberate, baroque vandalism — with the precision of a forger who's already burned the original. The messy, human truths, all the grit and struggle and blood in the teeth... smoothed over into neat, consumable fiction.

And God help him, there was a part of him that wanted it. Wanted a single, coherent lie — something he could rest inside without the constant tearing of then and now. As the thought took root, a slow warmth crept into his chest. Like the air itself had leaned in to comfort him. That was when he flinched. The Fade. Touching him. Stroking his mind like a hand through hair. A lullaby, low and poisonous.

He caught himself rubbing the bridge of his nose again, hard enough to leave a dent, as if the pressure might clear the fog.

The days blurred. Endless tabs open — historical archives, journals, news feeds — all agreeing on the same rewritten world. The internet, the last place he'd trusted for cold, factual truth, now humming like a printing press for the Fade's fabrications. Outside, the city shifted while nobody blinked. A bookstore he'd known for thirty years, gone. Replaced overnight by a glass-and-chrome tech start-up, sky reflected in angles too clean, too bright. Nobody noticed. Nobody cared.

Once, he caught himself humming. A tune he didn't recognise — cheerful, idiotic. It made his teeth itch. And yet... it was warm. Safe.

Lena wasn't doing better. After her collapse during the peer review session, they'd dressed her dismissal up as a "mandatory leave of absence." Her career, in other words, was over. Lily's teddy bear had practically fused to her hand, the stuffing poking through at one seam. She'd started humming too — the same lullaby? — eyes half-closed like it was a prayer.

"I dreamt of her last night," she told him, voice as thin as gauze. "She was laughing. And I... I was happy. Really happy. I wish I could stay there. It's so much easier than this."

The Fade was making her *want* it. Building a love she could drown in. A phantom motherhood that could eat her alive from the inside out, until the grief felt more real than the life she'd had before.

Then came Beethoven.

Alistair had switched on the classical station, searching for something to hold onto. The opening of the Fifth —

sharp, defiant — filled the room. He knew every note. Then the announcer slid in, voice smooth as glass:

"That was the magnificent *Symphony of Resolve* by Ludwig van Beethoven, composed during his exile in the Americas..."

Alistair's hand froze above the dial. Exile? Beethoven had never...

The rest of the sentence blurred under the roar in his ears. He lunged for his laptop. Wikipedia, biographies, music journals — they all said the same thing. Beethoven in Brazil. Beethoven, political exile. Deafness downgraded to a footnote. The man whose defiance had been born from silence now re-written as a tropical patriot with perfect hearing.

Something inside Alistair buckled. Beethoven had been a mirror — the fight against physical ruin, against fate itself — and now even *that* had been scrubbed clean.

The low hum from his computer speakers swelled, almost approving. He slammed his fist on the desk. "No! This isn't right!"

He called Lena. "It's Beethoven. They've gutted him. Changed everything."

She was quiet long enough that he thought the line had dropped. Then: "Van Gogh too. New exhibition. Court painter for the Dutch monarchy. They're calling him the Sun King's Painter." She gave a short, hollow laugh. "What's next? Shakespeare ghostwriting for Coca-Cola?"

The image made him nauseous. Van Gogh, whose brushstrokes bled with madness and hunger, now reduced to a docile ornament in velvet halls.

"It's targeting the foundations," Lena said, her tone gone flat, scientific. "If it can rewrite them — the people we tell stories about, the lives that give us meaning — it can rewrite anything. Genius, inspiration, the whole point of human struggle. All smoothed out."

Outside, the world looked the same. But it wasn't. People quoted Beethoven's exile like it was common knowledge. They smiled while doing it.

Alistair glanced at the glyph on his screen. Its pulse had changed — slower, deeper. Like breathing. Watching. Waiting.

The visions came again. Himself as philosopher in a garden with Clara. Himself painting Brazilian landscapes. Each one beautiful, peaceful... almost unbearable in their pull.

He reached across the table for Lena's hand. Her grip was solid. Too solid for someone fading.

"We can't let it win," he said.

It came out like a prayer. Or a promise. Or maybe a lie.

Chapter 12: The Rewritten Cosmos

The "Perpetual Oscillation Theory" wouldn't leave him alone. It sat there in his skull, ticking like some broken metronome — no beginning, no end, just the universe endlessly folding back on itself. Revision upon revision.

Too easy to see himself in it. His own life, rewritten over and over until the original was just... gone.

The whispers came more often now. Clara in the painter's studio, Clara in the philosopher's garden. Her hand warm in his. The Fade's voice, velvet and persistent: *stay here... stay here with me*. Not dreams anymore, but whole parallel lives, tailored for his comfort.

God help him, he wanted them. Any of them. Just one coherent lie that didn't hurt to live in.

Warmth bloomed in his chest. Too deliberate to be natural, like the air itself was leaning down to nudge him toward surrender. He jerked back from it, heart thudding. The Fade — stroking him, quiet as a cat.

His fingers moved on their own, tracing patterns in the condensation on his water glass. Little circles. A grounding ritual. Something to remind him he still had hands, still had *now*.

Outside, the city kept dancing its silent architectural ballet. Only now the changes weren't whispers — they were entire shouts. Blocks remapped overnight. Streets that led somewhere different than they had yesterday. Where a park had been, a towering monument now stood — mossy, weathered, as if it had always been there. People walked past it like they'd grown up under its shadow.

He stood in the middle of a reworked street, trying to map the old route in his head. Failed. The new one already felt natural. Which was maybe the worst part.

The air was thin. Humming. A low vibration under his shoes that he couldn't un-hear once he'd noticed it. And all around, the gentle background noise of people quietly readjusting to things they didn't remember being different.

Lena was further adrift every day. The teddy bear never left her arms — Lily's, in the life that wasn't. Her voice softened into the register people use when they're talking to children or ghosts.

"Lily asked me about the stars last night," she murmured, eyes not really here. "She wanted to know if they ever die. Or just... change. I told her they change. Always changing."

The words hit him like a dropped stone. She'd handed the Fade its own cosmology, wrapped in maternal comfort.

Her mind wasn't being broken; it was being bent into something pliant.

In desperation, Alistair reached for bedrock — philosophy. The Enlightenment. The big guns. Locke, Rousseau, Voltaire, Kant. His shelf groaned under their weight.

He dragged down *The Age of Reason: A Philosophical Compendium*. The cover was familiar, the spine cracked in places he'd read to pieces. He opened to Locke, ready to drink in his old anchor points.

But Locke was wrong.

Or rather, Locke was... different.

The words on the page were still cool and precise, but they carried an entirely new heartbeat: collective good above personal liberty. The necessity — not the danger — of centralized authority. Duty over choice. Submission as virtue.

A slow, ice-water dread spread through him.

He tore more books from the shelf. Rousseau's *Social Contract* now praising a benevolent state that would guide citizens to their "true" destiny — whether they agreed or not. Voltaire defending limited speech in the name of harmony. Kant reshaped into a preacher for the moral will of the state.

Every page hummed faintly, like the sound was coming from inside his own skull, urging him to accept, to nod along.

It felt like being pickpocketed, but the thing stolen was invisible until it was gone.

The Enlightenment wasn't a dawn anymore. It was a long afternoon nap in the lap of an all-knowing parent.

He slammed the books shut and went online, searching like a drowning man reaching for air. Every archive, every university database, every blog — all matched the rewrites. The old ideals weren't missing; it was as though they'd never existed.

He called Lena. "It's the Enlightenment. Locke, Rousseau, Voltaire — they've been rewritten. It's not about freedom anymore. It's about control."

On the other end, silence. Then her voice, so tired it sounded like it might dissolve mid-word. "I've seen it in my patients. People who'd have died on a hill for their independence now talking about 'the greater good' like it's scripture. They're not faking it, Alistair. They believe it. And the thing is... it feels right."

He closed his eyes. That was the danger. That it *did* feel right.

The Fade wasn't just tilting history; it was turning the compass that told you where right even was.

On his desk, the glyph pulsed. Slow. Satisfied.

Visions bled in around the edges — him, in some gentler timeline, giving speeches on the beauty of collective harmony. Clara at his side, serene, proud.

It was all so coherent. So stable. So easy.

The Fade didn't want him to forget; it wanted him to *choose.*

He reached blindly for Lena's hand. Found it. Gripped it harder than he meant to.

"We're still here," he said. His voice wasn't steady. "We have to be."

Chapter 13: The Fading Enlightenment

The "Perpetual Oscillation Theory" wouldn't leave his head. Not just a thought — more like a pulse, a low, insistent rhythm somewhere behind his eyes. This was the new cosmic truth, the one that had shoved the Big Bang out of the picture. A universe with no birth, no death. Just loops. Revisions. Over and over.

It was too close to home. A perfect metaphor for what his own life had become — the constant overwriting, the blurring of who he was, the steady erasure of himself.

The Fade's whispers had been background noise for weeks, but now they were crowding in, thick as fog. Clara's laughter from another life. The scent of turpentine in a sunlit painter's studio. The weight of a philosophy book in his lap as they sat in a walled garden. These weren't just passing fancies anymore — they'd taken on the solidity of memory, each one a carefully customised escape hatch from the gnawing dissonance of here and now.

And God, the pull was strong. He could feel it in his bones — the longing for just one neat, consistent lie to live inside. Any lie, so long as it ended this sickening clash of realities.

It began in his chest: a faint, almost pleasant warmth, as if the air itself had shifted to cradle him. A silent nudge to give in. He knew what it was — the Fade, reaching in, matching its grip to his private longing. A lullaby in poison form.

He caught himself gnawing at the inside of his cheek, hard enough to taste iron. A small, stupid anchor to the present.

The city was still dancing its strange, silent ballet, but the choreography had changed. No more subtle sleights of hand — now it was whole streets gone, entire blocks reimagined. Parks paved over for hulking monuments that looked centuries old, their stone scarred and weathered, as if they'd always been there.

People strolled past without a blink. As if they'd grown up with these buildings. As if none of it had been rewritten in front of their eyes.

He drifted through it like a ghost. This was his city, but it wasn't. Brick by brick, the familiar was being swapped out for something he didn't recognise.

The air felt thinner too. It carried a hum — so faint he might have imagined it — a low vibration under his shoes, as if the pavement itself were breathing. At crosswalks, he would stop and feel his brain try to remember the old way the streets ran, only for the new map to settle in just as easily. That was the worst part — how natural the changes felt once they were in place.

Some people still muttered in public about odd inconsistencies in recent events, like background static under the city's strange new harmony. But even those voices were getting quieter.

Lena was further adrift every day. The tether between them — between her and the real — was thinning to a thread.

The bear never left her arms now. Lily's bear. She held it tight like it could protect her from losing the child completely, though the child had never been real to begin with.

Her speech was full of "remember when" stories. Scraped knees. Bedtime rituals. The muffled giggle of a whispered secret in the dark.

Her eyes... they used to cut through anything. Now they drifted past him, softened by a grief that had no true cause.

"Lily asked me about the stars last night," she said one evening, barely above a whisper. Her gaze was fixed beyond the window, somewhere only she could see. "She wanted to know if they ever die, or if they just... change. I told her they just change. Always changing. Like everything else."

Her words lodged under his ribs. For a moment he almost envied her — the comfort of surrendering to a beautiful lie. But he knew what it was. The Fade had wrapped its fingers around that mother-love, reshaping it into a leash. She was being coaxed into her own erasure.

When he couldn't take it anymore, Alistair went back to bedrock. Philosophy.

He wanted something solid. Untouched. Something the Fade couldn't twist. The Enlightenment — surely that would hold.

He pictured the names as he walked to the shelves. Locke. Rousseau. Voltaire. Kant. Men whose ideas had set fire to entire centuries.

He muttered to himself as he pulled down *The Age of Reason: A Philosophical Compendium*, the habit of someone with fewer and fewer people to speak to. The book was as it had always been — cracked spine, worn corners.

But inside...

The Locke chapter should have been familiar — natural rights, government by consent, the sanctity of the individual. Instead he read about the primacy of the collective good. About how liberty must be balanced with — no, guided by — a strong, central authority.

A philosophy of quiet submission.

His pulse went hot and fast.

Rousseau's *Social Contract* had been altered too. Still about the general will, yes — but now it bent toward a benevolent, paternal state. Sacrifice autonomy, it said, for the true destiny of the collective.

Voltaire, once a champion of free speech, now argued for "managed discourse" — dissent only when it strengthened harmony. Censorship as civic duty.

Kant... even Kant... had been recast. The categorical imperative now served the needs of the state, not the conscience of the individual.

It was all still clever, all still internally consistent — just... wrong.

And underneath it, faint but constant, was that hum again, like a note held in the skull, making these warped ideas feel reasonable.

He checked the internet — academic archives, philosophy databases, popular explainer sites. All of them matched the new texts. Not one trace of the originals.

He rang Lena.

"Lena, it's the Enlightenment," he said, voice cracking in a way he didn't care to hide. "They've changed it. Locke, Rousseau, Voltaire... they're all saying the opposite. They're preaching control. Compliance. It's like they're remodelling the world into some kind of... docile utopia."

A pause. Then her sigh, heavy enough to sag through the line.

"I've seen it in my patients," she said. "People who used to bristle at any hint of authority now talk about the 'greater good' like it's gospel. They want oversight. They want their choices vetted. And they believe it — it's not forced. It's in them now."

She was quiet for a moment, then: "It's insidious, isn't it? Because it feels... right."

His stomach dropped. The Fade wasn't just undoing history or science. It was rewriting the very principles that made them human.

On his desk, the glyph's glow was stronger, its rhythm slow and steady, like a thing alive. The whispers in his mind spun new memories — not of resisting, but of standing in lecture halls, persuading others of the beauty of collective obedience. Clara in the front row, smiling.

These weren't temptations anymore. They were rehearsals.

The Fade didn't want him to forget. It wanted him to choose.

The choice felt like a slow fall. And maybe it always had been.

He reached for Lena's hand. They held on — not tight, just steady. Two people clinging to a moment that still belonged to them.

"We're still here, Lena," he said. His voice sounded raw, but steady. "We're still us. We have to be."

Chapter 14: Echoes of a Borrowed Life

Enlightenment. Twisted into a gospel of benevolent control. It kept looping in Alistair's head, like a splinter he couldn't dig out. If they could rewrite *that* — the very bones of human freedom — what chance did one memory have? One fragile, slippery self?

The Fade's whispers didn't sit politely in the background anymore. They barged in, bright and vivid, dragging Clara into the room — her hand warm on his cheek, paint on her fingers. The studio's windows thrown open to sea air. A philosopher's garden, the sunlight dappled on worn stone. Not dreams. Not even visions. Full-blown *lives*, each tugging at him with its own gravity.

He could feel the strain physically now — the constant ache behind his eyes, the tremor in his hands that never quite stopped. Bone-deep exhaustion. The kind that doesn't fade after a night's sleep.

Then the warmth. Always the warmth. Creeping through his chest, gentle, persuasive, like the air itself was trying to cradle him. An invitation he could almost fall into. Almost.

He bit down on his lip, hard. Copper flooded his mouth. A taste from childhood — when chewing his lip was how he got through math exams, or awkward silences. It kept him here. Just barely.

Outside, the city was a moving painting that couldn't make up its mind.

A sleek monorail slid through the air now, silver cars gliding silently where the market used to shout and clatter. The spices, the shouting vendors, the mess of colour — gone. Steel and glass in their place. And nobody seemed to notice.

People moved under those clean, alien lines like it had always been this way. He searched their faces for some sign of disbelief. Found none.

The air felt thinner. Hummed, even. Low, steady. Like the ground itself was vibrating.

At crosswalks, he'd blink and see two cities overlaid — the one he remembered and the one that had replaced it. A shiver of disorientation, then it passed, and the new one felt normal again. That was the part that scared him most: how quickly the lies settled in.

Sometimes, in the background of street noise, he'd catch fragments — people quietly disagreeing on what had happened last week, what a street used to be called. That undercurrent was getting softer. Fading out.

Lena was almost gone.

The bear was welded to her arms now. Lily's bear. She held it like a shield against grief — grief that had no source in this reality but clung to her anyway.

Her voice was a museum of small memories. Lily's scraped knees. Bedtime whispers. The warmth of a small body falling asleep on hers.

Once, she hummed a tune. "Lily loved this song," she said, smiling faintly. "She'd twirl until she fell over laughing."

It was too real. Even he could almost see her — the little girl who'd never existed.

He could feel how the Fade had laced this false child into Lena's marrow, offering her something he couldn't: comfort.

A drawing on the fridge — a stick figure with a balloon — gave off the faintest glow. Just enough to make Lena's eyes soften, to lock the fiction in place.

Then it was his turn.

The past didn't just bend. It accelerated.

One morning, he woke with a whole marriage in his head. Not Sarah — the linguist whose death had blown open this nightmare. Not Clara — the quiet philosopher in her sea-cottage.

This time it was Eleanor. Dark curls, determined eyes. An architect. Together they'd built a design firm, stayed up late over blueprints, breathed in sawdust and fresh plaster. He remembered their fights, their reconciliations. The warm weight of her hand in his.

It was so *tactile* it scared him.

He went straight to the study. Found his wedding album. The cover — different. Modern. Inside, there they were: a younger him, arm around Eleanor, smiling in a way that hurt to look at.

Not the church where he'd married Sarah, but a white-walled art gallery. Guests he didn't know.

He could almost feel Eleanor beside him. And the photo... it hummed. Just enough to blur the edges of Sarah.

Sarah. Clara. Eleanor.

Each version of him with them felt whole. Complete. Emotionally airtight.

He couldn't move. The urge to rip the album apart, to break the spell — it was there, but his arms felt heavy, like they belonged to someone else.

He tried calling Ben Carter. Ben, who'd sat with him through the worst of Sarah's absence. He needed to hear him confirm the truth.

Voicemail. Again. Again.

Finally, a text.

Alistair?.. Who is this?.. I think you have the wrong number. My name's Ben Harrison. We met once at a philosophy conference in Edinburgh. You gave a... controversial talk on Kant.

His chest went hollow.

So now he was the *philosopher* Alistair, married to Clara. And the text dragged in a Marcus Thorne — a friend from another newly minted life.

The Fade wasn't just swapping memories. It was cutting his ties, one by one, until there was no one left who remembered him the way he remembered himself.

He dropped into his desk chair, face in his hands. The sound that came out of him was barely a sob. “This is it. I’m losing everyone. I’m losing me.”

Lena’s work was filling up with worse cases.

Not just new memories — new selves.

The shy man who woke up loud and gregarious. The devout woman who opened her eyes an atheist, burning with conviction. None of them felt the seam. To them, they’d always been this way.

“It’s not psychosis,” she told him flatly one evening. “It’s... re-calibration. The Fade isn’t just editing the past. It’s rewriting the soul.”

Her voice dropped. “Sometimes I look in the mirror and I don’t know which me I’m looking at. Lily’s mother. Or the one who only had her research. I can’t tell which one’s the lie.” She gave a laugh with no humour in it.

The glyph on his desk pulsed, smug.

The whispers were busy now — not just dangling Clara or Eleanor, but showing him childhoods he’d never had, parents he’d never known, careers he’d never chosen.

A factory worker’s son. A painter. An archaeologist. Each version complete, saturated with feeling.

And again — the warmth. The gentle pull to stop fighting.

He knew the Fade's touch by now.

It didn't just want him to forget. It wanted him to *become*. To slide into one of its ready-made lives until the original him dissolved entirely.

The thought was too big to fight. Too big to even hold for long.

He reached for Lena's hand. Their fingers interlocked. A last point of contact.

"We're all we have left," he told her. His voice was wrecked but steady. "Don't let go."

Chapter 15: The Fractured Reflection

It didn't slow. Not for a heartbeat.

Linguist. Philosopher. Painter. Architect. Engineer's boy. Crofter's boy. Historian. Diplomat. Husband to Sarah—then Clara—then Eleanor—then Beatrice.

They pressed in like a crowd in a narrow stairwell, every life elbowing for space, each with its own smell and weather and private ache. Each airtight. Each certain.

The first Alistair—the one who had stood by Sarah's grave and walked home with that ringing emptiness in his chest—kept getting smaller. A thin echo under the loudness of the others. If he turned his head too fast inside himself, he could almost miss the original completely.

The Fade had stopped purring. It pushed. It stitched these lives together with tidy little seams, told a story where he'd always been all of them, some fluid creature who shifted and forgot and called that survival.

It hurt in ordinary ways and in ways he didn't have names for. The ache behind his eyes had settled into something permanent, a dull pressure like weather. His hands trembled even at rest. Sleep no longer mattered; if he dozed for three hours or ten minutes, he woke carrying the same weight.

And then the warmth. That thin bloom under the sternum, rising like steam on a cold morning. A softness that meant surrender.

He knew that touch now. The Fade's hand.

He bit his lower lip until copper spilled onto his tongue. It grounded him, just. He blinked at the desk. A sandwich sat there, half eaten, edges drying out. He tried to remember making it and found only blank hallway in his mind.

Outside, the city had been edited again.

Where the market used to thicken the air with cumin, frying oil, wet stone, there was a monorail—sleek, frictionless cars sliding past, reflections moving like fish along the glass towers. The place that had once bumped your elbow with someone else's basket now hummed at a higher, colder pitch.

And nobody looked surprised.

Faces lifted to the passing cars wore the placid recognition of habit. Feet found new routes like they'd been walking them since childhood.

The air itself seemed thinner, as if something had siphoned the weight out of it. A low tremor ran up through the pavement into his ankles when he stood at the curb—like a speaker turned down but never off.

He tried, for form's sake, to sketch the old street in his head—the slant of the awnings, the chipped cornices, the soap-slick from the butcher's drain. But the new map clicked into place just as neatly. That was the coldest part: his mind accommodating the edit, smoothing the splice so the cut vanished.

Occasionally, at a café table or a crossing, he'd hear two people murmur a correction—no, it was on Wednesday, not Tuesday; no, her name was Marta—but even that static was thinning. The city was learning its new lines.

Lena was slipping faster.

Lily's teddy—threadbare beige with one flattened ear—lived between her elbow and ribcage now, a permanent fixture. She held it like an amulet against a grief that this world didn't officially contain.

Her sentences arrived wrapped in small domestic scenes. Skinned knees. Milk moustaches. A whisper at the crack of a bedroom door: still awake?

One afternoon she hummed, absentmindedly, circling the same eight notes.

"Lily loved this," she said to the bear, not to him. "She'd twirl until she fell over laughing."

The way her mouth softened made something twist in him. He could almost see the child—dark hair sticking with sweat, socks sliding on the kitchen tile, laughter hitting that high glassy edge only kids manage.

The Fade had grown her so deep in Lena's marrow that it warmed the whole room.

He noticed the drawing on her fridge only because the colors were too saturated—sun-yellow, sky-blue, a stick figure with a lopsided smile. For a second, he thought the paper gave off a faint heat against his palm. Not possible. Still—he didn't touch it again.

Then the wheel turned, and it was his turn to be altered.

A new wife arrived like weather rolling in.

Not Sarah.

Not Clara.

Not Eleanor.

Beatrice.

Historian. Quiet as snowfall, fierce as flint. Their life together assembled itself fully formed: mornings in reading rooms where you had to sign your name in pencil; afternoons hunting marginalia; nights of tea gone cold beside open folios. The musk of parchment. The chalk squeak of a graphite line on tracing paper. The hush you keep out of respect for the dead voices you're handling.

He felt the ghost-weight of her wedding band against his palm when he reached for her. There was no one there. The warmth still lingered.

He walked to the study and found an album he didn't recognize by shape alone—plain cloth cover, academic and humorless. He set it on the table and opened to the first page. There he was: thinner, eyes brighter, hair un-streaked. The woman beside him wore a neat bun and looked like she'd already read three books that morning. Chapel pews and stone. No one he recognized in the aisle, and yet—the curve of his arm around her waist had the unconsciousness of habit. His smile—the complicated kind—hurt to look at.

The photograph hummed, almost too soft to register. He felt the old memory of Sarah step one pace back.

Sarah. Clara. Eleanor. Beatrice.

All true. None true.

He wanted to tear the page out with both hands and couldn't make his fingers move.

He called Ben Carter because that was the thing you did when you couldn't trust your own head—he'd learned that once and should have been able to remember it forever. Voicemail caught him three times. He texted with a bluntness that felt like panic.

The reply came as if from another house on another street.

Alistair?.. Who is this?.. I think you have the wrong number. My name's Ben Harrison. We met once at a philosophy conference. You spoke about Kant. Mentioned your wife, Clara. Are you still in touch with Marcus Thorne? And didn't you marry a historian named Beatrice for a while?..

Cold ran through him in a thick sheet. It settled. He couldn't shake it.

Ben—deleted. Clara—spliced in. Marcus—stitched. Beatrice—fresh thread.

The Fade wasn't just drafting new chapters; it was pulling up the old floorboards, cutting the joists, salting the soil.

He sat, hard, and put his hands over his face. The words came out thin. "This is it," he said to the room. "I'm losing everyone. I'm losing me."

Lena's case notes kept changing, too, except she hadn't changed them.

Not memories—selves.

The shy man who had taken three sessions to meet her eyes came in laughing and loud, knees wide, voice booming, and swore he'd always been the one to speak first. The woman who had brought a rosary to every appointment arrived with a calm, hard certainty that God was a tool for frightened minds. If she missed the beads, her face didn't show it.

No one felt the seam.

"It's a recalibration," Lena said into her hands one evening, her voice oddly flat, like she'd scraped it clean of tone. "Not psychosis. The Fade's changing the soul." She laughed once, without warmth. "They don't even know. Some of them think I'm the problem."

She looked at the mirror over his shoulder, not at herself but through the idea of herself. "Sometimes I see Lily's mother. Sometimes I see the woman who chose data over everything. I can't tell which is the lie."

Back home, the glyph on his desk pulsed with the lazy confidence of a metronome that knows you'll follow it. Every few seconds, a thread of light reached and curled back.

The voices in his head were busy at their workbench. New childhoods slid into place—one with damp flats that smelled of fried onions and engine oil; one with rooms small as pockets but windows that opened to heather. New parents, strict or laughing. New apprenticeships, new letters after his name, new hands to hold.

Painter. Archaeologist. Factory worker's son.

Each set of memories had texture—the pinch of a collar, the oil under the thumbnail, the weight of a brush at wrist—because that's how you convince a body.

And the warmth kept returning, a careful arm across his shoulders.

This wasn't only about subtraction. The Fade wanted him to become. To be something agreeable and complete. To settle into the harmonized chord and call it truth.

He was tired. The kind of tired that folds you, that tempts you to lay down wherever you happen to be and let the floor decide.

He reached for Lena's hand across the desk. Her fingers were cold and strong; his were shaking.

"We're all we have left," he said. The words fuzzed at the edges but the center held. "Don't let go."

Chapter 16: The Rewritten World Order

The city had a new spine and refused to admit it.

Sleek cars slid along the sky-rail, whisper-quiet where the old market used to bark and jostle and smell like cumin and old rain. Glass where there'd been peeling paint. Polished chrome where there'd been dented shutters and a grumpy grocer who short-changed everyone evenly. And nobody blinked. Acceptance moved through the streets like clean water. He watched a bearded man in a suit lift his arm to check a watch that had never existed yesterday and then step onto a platform that had always been here—apparently.

Alistair stood at the window and tried to force the old street back into place. The red awning over the fishmonger. The wobbling bicycle chained to a drainpipe. Sticky pavement where the fig cart tipped that one summer. His mind offered the new map instead, crisp as a blueprint. It landed with a click that made his stomach turn.

The ache behind his eyes had become a roommate. His hands trembled just enough to make pouring coffee an act of faith. He kept catching himself with his jaw locked so hard his ears rang. Every time he loosened it, that faint warmth rose in his chest, thin as breath blown across the neck of a bottle. The Fade's hand, coaxing. He gritted his teeth and let copper bloom on his tongue.

Lena drifted in and out with the bear. Lily's bear. The cheap stitching on the paw coming loose, one ear mashed flat by sleep that had never happened. She held it as if a child might appear if she kept her arms ready.

"She hated peas," Lena told the kitchen light, soft and fond. "Used to line them up on the edge of the plate like little soldiers and flick them at me one by—" She paused, smiled at nothing. "She thought I didn't notice."

He stared at the drawing on her fridge—purple sun in the wrong corner, a house with seven windows and a lopsided heart. The paper gave off the faintest warmth, like it remembered a hand pressing hard with a crayon. He half-expected to see fingerprints impressed in the wax.

"I almost hear her feet," Lena said. "That patter, you know?" She hummed a tune he didn't know and the room leaned toward it. For a breath, he almost did too. That scared him more than anything.

The Fade came for him through love again. It had a talent for that.

Beatrice arrived as if she'd stepped out of a library stack: ink-smudged fingers, hair pinned with careless efficiency, a voice that could turn a footnote into a secret. The first image was a narrow chapel with bad floral arrangements. He couldn't name a single guest, and yet the angle of his own grin—crooked, real—made his throat ache.

He took the album down. It was heavier than it looked, bound in plain cloth, humming faintly in his hands like an old transformer. There they were on the step, confetti like torn syllables in the air. He could smell cool stone and old lilies; he could feel the press of her shoulder. The photo warmed under his thumbs. His memory of Sarah shifted a millimetre back, not erased—re-shelved.

He called Ben because that's what you do when the room is tilting. Straight to voicemail. Again. He set the phone down, picked it up, tried the number with the old country code like a superstition. Nothing. Then the reply:

Alistair?.. Who is this?.. Think you have the wrong number. I'm Ben Harrison. We met at the Edinburgh Kant conference—you mentioned your wife, Clara. Are you still in touch with Marcus Thorne? And didn't you marry a historian named Beatrice for a while?..

The floor dropped an inch. He sat before he fell. Ben Carter was gone. Clara had been slotted in cleanly. Marcus slid into place like a chess piece. His breath went shallow, as if oxygen now carried terms and conditions.

At Lena's clinic, reality arrived dressed as professionalism. Her notes stayed neat even while the truth bled through them. A shy man walked in and left with a booming laugh he claimed he'd always had. A woman crossed herself at the door on Tuesday and argued theology from an atheist's certainty on Friday, quoting authors she swore she'd always loved. No seams, no stitches showing. The before had never existed. The after wore the same face.

"It's recalibration," Lena said, flat and precise, as if the word might keep panic from cracking her voice. "Not delusion. It's... *compliance*, written into the self." She touched the bear's ear, smoothed it back. "Some mornings I swear I'm only a researcher who resents children. And some mornings Lily's mother looks out of my eyes. I don't know which is the lie. Or if the question still means anything."

He watched her mouth try to smile. It didn't quite happen.

Back at his desk, the glyph pulsed with a patient, smug pulse, like a lighthouse for the wrong coast. New childhoods spooled in him with the authority of old wounds: the factory's oil-slick air; the blunt pride of a crofter's hands; the philosopher's certainty when Clara laughed at a well-placed question; Eleanor's pencil tapping out a rhythm for a load-bearing wall. All of it crisp, all of it felt.

The warmth started again under his breastbone. He pressed knuckles there until it faded.

The Fade didn't want to strip him. It wanted to *complete* him—in the way a museum "completes" a statue with a modern replacement limb. Seamless from a distance. False up close. He could feel the urge to accept it rise like sleep. He was so tired.

He reached for Lena's hand. Their fingers fitted like a remembered motion. "We're all we've got," he said, voice scraped thin. "Don't—" He couldn't finish.

"I won't," she said. For now, it held.

Chapter 17: The Echo Chamber of Truth

There were days when the inside of his head sounded like a crowded station—the announcer calling destinations in voices that all belonged to him.

Linguist. Philosopher. Painter. Architect. Engineer's boy. Crofter's boy. Historian. Diplomat. Husband to Sarah, then Clara, then Eleanor, then Beatrice. All the trains arrived on time. None of them left.

Each life used the same body differently. The philosopher stood taller; the painter carried colour in the wrist; the diplomat's handshakes had weight. He could feel it all. He could make it convincing enough to step into. That was the worst of it.

The Fade's chorus wasn't soft anymore. It patted the seat beside it and made room for yet another story, then pressed that story down into the sediment of him until it felt older than yesterday. It stitched the titles together into one long spine where he had always been everyone. It called that *coherence.* He called it erasure.

The ache behind his eyes had gained edges. He pressed his thumbs to his sockets and saw starbursts. The tremor in his fingers turned writing into a careful art, cups into hazards. The bone-deep tiredness had lost the habit of letting sleep help. And when he let his guard slip for a second, the room exhaled that pleasant warmth again, humming like a fridge at midnight. Surrender was made of soft things, not hard ones.

He stood at the window until the glass remembered his breath. The new monorail cut clean lines through a sky that didn't seem to remember clouds. The old market's noise came only when he closed his eyes on purpose. When he opened them, people moved with the confidence of long practice across platforms that had existed since there were platforms. He tried to be angry at them. But there was nothing to be angry at. They had nothing to compare with.

He closed his eyes and saw the old layout. Opened them and felt the new one settle in with that same awful click. His own mind was doing the Fade's work for it—the way a tongue keeps worrying a cracked tooth.

Lena was losing the thread differently. The bear rode her hip; the lullaby lived in her throat now like a second pulse. She spoke in small details, the kind you don't invent: a chipped mug with a frog on it; the way Lily wiped her hands on her skirt and then pretended she hadn't; a whispered "again" at the end of a story.

"Lily loved this," she said, humming that tune again. He didn't know it, but the bear seemed to. Her eyes softened along its seams. He wished he could hate the tenderness. He managed only envy for its certainty.

He noticed the glow of the crayon drawing again. It wasn't bright. It just felt... warm when he stood near it, like the paper had a pulse. The Fade didn't need to argue with you if it could hum you into agreement.

They began to trip over each other's truths. He would say "the bakery on Harrow," and she would tilt her head: "There's never been a bakery on Harrow; you mean the municipal gallery." He would insist on a professor's name; she would provide the correct replacement with a frown, the way you correct the tense in a sentence. Careful, patient, worried for him. He started to hear the word *delusional* tucked under the end of her sentences even when she didn't say it.

He went for something big. Something anchor-heavy.

"Berlin Wall," he said. "November ninth, 1989. Hammers. People on shoulders. The concrete looked like stale bread when it broke." He mimed the swing because sometimes your body convinces people better than your mouth.

She considered him like a problem that could be solved with the right equation. "There was a treaty. Early nineties. Gradual de-escalation. No single fall." Her voice was gentle, professional, dangerous. "You're thinking of the 'Spirit of Unity' docu-drama they made as a symbolic capstone. It used the imagery to—"

The air itself hummed approval. His memory suddenly felt like a clumsy prop in the wrong play.

"But the footage—" He heard the break in his voice and hated it. "It was *news*, Lena. People cried. I cried." He hit his fist too softly against the table and wished it had hurt.

She looked at him with a tenderness that made his skin want to crawl off his bones. Maternal. "You're exhausted," she said. "Brains make films when they're tired. They edit. They add music." She reached for his hand and the room warmed. "You don't have to hold all of that. It's hurting you."

He pulled his hand back. The warmth faded, and with it the urge to say *Fine, I'll forget*.

Rage flickered—bright, then gone. He was too tired to feed it.

The glyph on his screen pulsed like a heartbeat he had accidentally matched his to. The visions came clean as print: the factory in morning heat; Clara's laugh under an oak; Brazil's ferocious greens smeared into paint; Eleanor's pencil carving a museum out of air; the moor's wind roughing the inside of his lungs; Beatrice's desk with its splayed notebooks; Marcus's careful hands measuring the shape of a compromise. None of it wobbled. Each life offered a coherent story and a soft landing. He understood the temptation the way you understand a bed at 4 a.m.

The Fade didn't want a blank slate. It wanted a palimpsest you couldn't tell had ever been scraped.

He squeezed Lena's hand until their knuckles went bloodless. "We're it," he said. "You and me. No one else remembers us right."

She nodded, eyes glossy. "Then we remember each other."

He went home and did the mean, stubborn thing: opened old files that hurt to look at. The Andean cave photos weren't beautiful. They were awkward. Shadows where there shouldn't have been shadows. But something tooth-true hid in the mess. He stopped reading them as language. Treated them like waveforms. He mapped the frequencies. He tracked the shifts they predicted. The lines coincided too often to be luck.

"To cleanse. To prepare. For the next cycle."

Not poetry. Instruction. The glyphs weren't telling—they were *doing*. A program written in a syntax nobody had a right to know.

His stomach turned as if he'd swallowed ice. The Fade wasn't a storm; it was an operating system. And he'd clicked *Run*.

The patterns it favoured were tidy. Smoothing edges. Replacing ruptures with processes. Turning spikes into curves. It read like the minutes of a meeting where somebody said, "Can we make it less messy?" and the room nodded.

It fought back when resisted. Which meant it understood resistance and had already designed for it.

The screen brightened; the whispers sharpened: *You see it. Good. Come sit where it is easy.*

He put his fist into the desk hard enough to sting. "Not yet," he said, to the screen or to himself. "Not while I remember Sarah."

The room stayed warm. He let it be. He didn't let it in.

Chapter 18: The Unveiling Program

He stopped pretending the glyph was a text and admitted what it was: a console.

He told himself to prove it like a scholar would. He did it like a man pulling wire out of a wall with his bare hands.

Line by line, he charted what changed when. The stars first—distances recalculated into something elegant and wrong. Then the big historical hinges—revolutions shaved down into reforms that left everyone with clean hands in the photographs. Then the small, private edits—marriages rearranged until love sat where it made the most narrative sense. He found the curves that predicted each correction. They were pretty. He hated them.

He talked to Lena less and sent her more— snapshots of patterns, little crescents of logic where the Fade's hand had hesitated. She sent back people—clients whose *selves* had been updated at two in the morning, their dreams suddenly compatible with a past that had never happened. They were both right. That was the problem.

Sleep came like a stranger knocking at the wrong door. He let it pass. Coffee shook in the cup. He bit his nails until the half moons bled. Somewhere in there he laughed at the triviality of that, then kept biting.

The city kept tidying itself. Bollards aligned. Timetables synchronized. Museums adopted new plaques with calm gratitude. In a café that had once been a hardware store, a girl learned a song Alistair had never heard and sang it to a man who cried because his mother had taught it to him when the wall came down slowly and peacefully over the course of diplomatic months. Consensus hardened like cooling glass.

He tried markers that should have been immovable. Dates. Dead languages. The location of a scar on his own wrist. The Fade moved around them the way water moves around stones— patient, unbothered, intent on rounding corners.

The warmth under his sternum would surge when he stared too long, and the ache along his arm would spike into small lightning when he got a line right. He learned to work through both. Pain could be a metronome. Comfort could be noise.

The breakthrough didn't feel like fireworks. It felt like hearing a key click a tumblers' worth of metal.

Buried in a nest of recursions, he found instruction that referred to itself, a loop that knew it was a loop. A meta-directive with teeth. The anti-sequence had been folded in; his paradox now sat like grit inside a well-oiled machine. The grit made a sound.

He mapped the sound. He mapped the moments the Fade flinched. There weren't many. There were enough.

When he pushed there, the room answered.

The air thickened. The glyph's light went frantic, all lines and shards. The walls took on the look of skin about to bruise. He felt the pressure—not metaphor now—clamp his ribs. And then the other thing: that vision he could not stop seeing arrived not as a flash, but as an environment.

No anchors. No past. No *after*. People lighting and unlacing in the same blink. Names that wouldn't hold their own letters. It wasn't darkness. It was exposure—an overexposed frame where nothing could develop. He felt his own edges trying to soften.

He grabbed for the desk. "Lena." His voice sounded like it had been dragged down stairs. "If we snap it— if we break it *all the way*—it's not reset. It's obliteration. Memory included. Static. Void."

Her face on the screen (he'd called without noticing) had gone the colour of paper. She nodded once, twice, as if agreeing with a diagnosis she hated. "I saw it too. It's a seal, Alistair. The lie is the lid. Whatever's under it is worse." She glanced off-camera, maybe at a drawing that glowed a little. "The Ancients didn't just erase. They *contained*."

He wanted to make a joke to stop the room from crushing him. Nothing rose. They both smiled anyway—thin, brittle. A reflex against collapse.

He stared at the glyph until his eyes watered. The dam metaphor arrived uninvited. The Fade was an ugly wall across a river that would otherwise eat the town. He had come with a sledgehammer because he hated dams. Now he could hear the roar beyond it and knew some of that sound wanted his bones.

The whispers changed register. They were no longer coaxing; they adjudicated: *The cycle is eternal. To break it is to break all.*

He didn't answer them. He reached for Lena instead. Their hands met halfway across different rooms the way lonely people do— with an object, with a word.

"Together," he said. It wasn't brave. It was the only sentence that still fit.

Her fingers tightened around the bear and the edge of her desk. "To the end," she said. "Whichever one."

They went back to work, because there wasn't anything else left that wasn't surrender. The hum of the Loom found a new pitch. He let it settle in his bones and pretended it was only electricity.

Outside, a train slid across a sky that refused to admit it had ever been otherwise. Inside, he traced a wound only the wound-giver felt. The hum of the Loom kept time in his bones, pretending to be nothing more than electricity.

He told himself they still had each other. But Lena's face on the darkened screen had already started to fade in his mind — not gone, not yet, but softened at the edges, like a photograph left too long in the sun.

That was how the Fade worked. Not with fire. With weather.

Chapter 19: The Architect of Oblivion

The Fade's whispers had changed. They no longer pressed against him from the outside; they bloomed from within, seeded in the softened edges of his thoughts. *You understand now. This is the way. This is the future. Surrender. Become one with the cycle. Forget the old. Embrace the new. It is peaceful. It is an order.*

The words carried that awful, measured calm. Not chaos. No, far worse — a deliberate architecture. Sentient. Ancient. A reformatting of reality itself, dressed up as purification.

He pictured himself small inside it — not metaphor-small, but *mouse in a small clockwork cathedral.* The gears so vast and patient, they barely noticed his scrambling, just felt the faint friction of his refusal. The guilt was a weight under his tongue, a constant, metallic bitterness: he had woken it.

He muttered something under his breath. Lately, he'd been doing that without realizing, a habit from when there'd been no one else left to talk to.

The glyph on the computer was still there, pulsing. Watching. Not watching — boring into him. The light seemed to go *through* his skin. His body started to shake, not from the tiredness (though the tiredness had dug deep into him) but from that deeper kind of fear that sits in the bones and tries to rattle its way out. A spike of pain bloomed behind his eyes, white-hot, rhythmic. He dropped into the old armchair, lungs working too hard, the air thick, sour, as if the Fade itself had seeped into the walls. His fingers dug into the fabric until the knuckles whitened. Something to hold. Something solid.

The voices showed him doors. Lives. He could walk through any one of them. The philosopher, calm and steady, accepting the turn of the cycle beside Clara, their hands resting together like stones in a river. The painter, somewhere sunlit, painting beauty that never rotted, never changed. Each life so neat. So tempting. A life without the jagged edges of the truth. He actually felt the ache of wanting it. But then he pictured Sarah. The actual Sarah, not a Fade-curated memory. The chipped cup on his table caught his eye — but even that, he realised, seemed... wrong. Its old pattern shifted when he wasn't looking, like it had decided to play along with the lie.

Outside, the city rearranged itself again. A bridge he'd crossed half his life now arched over a river much wider than it had ever been, flanked by strange plants blooming and rotting in the same breath. The noise had changed too — no more car-hum, just a deep, resonant throb under everything, the bass note of the Perpetual Oscillation Theory come alive. People moved like they'd been choreographed. Eyes empty. A woman stopped mid-step, gazed up at a brand-new spire, its peak glowing as if lit from the inside, and smiled like she'd been born under its shadow.

Lena was almost gone when he found her. Still in the same clothes, hair loose, clinging to Lily's teddy like it was the only thing keeping her upright. Her office smelled stale. Sweet, too, faintly, like the ghost of baby powder.

"Lily's sleeping," she said, soft as a lullaby. "She dreamt about the old world. Sharp edges, noise. I told her the new one's better. Safe. Clean." She looked at him then. Something in her eyes flickered — recognition, maybe — before the softness slid back over it. "You're so tired, Alistair. Why fight it? You could rest."

The Fade was speaking through her. He felt it in his gut. The little blank stutter in her pupils, like a screen flicker. He almost reached for her hand, then stopped — afraid that even a touch would pull him into that warm, false quiet.

"Do you remember the glyphs? The cave? *To cleanse. To prepare. For the next cycle*?" His voice cracked.

Her brow wrinkled for half a heartbeat. "Glyphs? No... my work's always been with children. Lily needs me." She looked back at the bear. The flicker was gone.

The Fade wasn't wasting time. It had a pattern: erase, pacify, overwrite. He'd seen it before — the history professor who ended up a loose pile of unconnected thoughts after resisting too long.

Back at his desk, the low thrum in his skull wouldn't let up. He told himself there had to be a counter-command. If he'd unlocked it with language, then there had to be an un-language, a kill sequence. He started digging for anti-patterns, inversions. His hands shook so hard he almost dropped the stylus. The apartment grew colder. Objects moved when he wasn't watching. The voice in his head shifted from coaxing to commanding: *You cannot resist. You are part of the program. Your defiance is an error. Be erased.*

The pain hit his left arm like a thousand pins driven in all at once. He gasped, clawing at it. No mark. The Fade had decided to skip persuasion.

He wiped the sweat from his face with the heel of his hand. Looked at Sarah's photo. Then the glyph. Then his hands again, still shaking. The fight wasn't just about himself anymore. It was about the right for anyone, ever, to remember the real thing, no matter how ugly it was.

"You won't take her," he said to the empty room, voice scraping raw. "You won't take me."

Chapter 20: The Loom of Lies

The pain in his arm wasn't just pain anymore. It had taught him. Found the fault lines in his nerves and worked them like a craftsman. Every time he pushed back against the Fade, the current would flare — white-hot, electric — as if the thing was inside the muscle, pulling the wire. It wasn't just a program now. That fiction had burned away days ago. It was *someone*. Or something close enough. And it was angry.

The voices were worse. No longer quiet, no longer just whispering from some hidden crack in his head. They crowded in, talking over each other, a thousand little hooks disguised as promises. Whole lives laid out for him — smooth, edited, painless — if only he'd stop. If only he'd hand himself over. His real self felt thin. Not just worn, but threadbare. A single fibre stretched to snapping, holding a whole tapestry together that the Fade kept tugging at.

He paced the apartment until his jaw ached from clenching. The carpet had a faint track in it now, a line worn between the desk and the kitchen that he didn't remember making. He leaned into the desk again, squinting through the blur. The glyph on the screen throbbed in time with the pulse of pain behind his eyes. Even the room felt wrong. The walls too close. The air too cold. That metallic tang never left anymore — somewhere between burnt wiring and ozone before a storm.

He'd glance away, and things would move. A pen rolling slow to the table's edge. A book sliding open to a page he was certain didn't exist yesterday, the text half-strange, bent just enough to mock him. Sometimes he'd curse at it — at the room, at the air — just to fill the silence.

Days became something else. Could've been weeks. Could've been hours stacked oddly. The only measure was how deep the lines on his face had carved themselves in the mirror, and how badly his hands shook. He lived on bitter coffee and that jittery thread of manic determination that doesn't feel like energy so much as survival. Fingers raw from tracing the same loops, looking for the one slip in the pattern.

When the Fade came now, it didn't always knock first. Sarah would be in his living room — not ghostly, but painfully solid — asking why he couldn't just stop. "Why won't you let me rest?" That voice undid him every time. The way her mouth moved around the words, the exact pitch. It made him think maybe he *was* cruel, keeping her here in this fight. And then she'd flicker, dissolve into static, and someone else would take her place — Clara, Eleanor, Beatrice — each one carrying a different key to peace, each turning it in the lock of his resolve. He'd reach for them, always too slow, always clutching at nothing.

He called Lena again. Straight to voicemail. Called the office. Knocked at her door. Nothing. Just that heavy silence. He didn't need to be told. He could see it: Lily woven so tightly into her, the Fade's quiet gift, the lie made so comfortable she wouldn't want to step out of it. The grief hit low, under the ribs, and stayed there.

Outside, the changes were past subtle now. Whole streets bent into different shapes. Landmarks replaced by black, humming structures that looked like they'd been grown rather than built, their surfaces bending light in ways that hurt to stare at. People moved like they'd rehearsed it. Faces blank in a way that felt too smooth. A boy — five, maybe — pointed up at the clouds, chattering about "the great Loom" like it was as ordinary as rain. His parents nodded. Smiled. The words were already inside them.

Back in the apartment, the pain in his arm ripped sideways into his chest. Breath wouldn't come properly. He folded to the floor, fingers digging at his ribs. Something unseen pressed down, steady and merciless. The chorus in his head was deafening now: *You are an error. You are a glitch. Be assimilated. Be corrected. Forget.*

And yet, under it — under the noise, under the hurt — something clicked. The glyphs. Not just loops but loops feeding themselves, a paradox nested like a trap inside the Fade's own syntax. An error it had buried in its perfection. A kill command hidden in plain sight. Dangerous as hell. If he'd read it wrong, it wouldn't just erase him. It'd erase the *possibility* of him.

He crawled to the desk, every joint screaming, vision fractured at the edges. His fingers rattled over the keys, fighting the weight pressing in on his lungs. The Fade knew. He could feel it pressing harder, turning the room's gravity up, trying to pin him to the floor. Sweat and tears blurred together on the desk's surface. Each symbol he typed was a memory — Sarah's hair falling across her face, her voice in the kitchen, the way she'd hum under her breath without knowing.

The final line blinked at him, waiting. The glyph on the screen flared, its light sharp enough to slice the room apart. The voices reached their pitch. *Surrender. Let go. Be free.*

He shut his eyes. One tear made it down, hot against the grime on his cheek. Sarah was there, steady and unaltered in his mind's eye. The warmth of her hand. The sound of her laughing at something too small to explain.

He hit the key.

Chapter 21: The Violent Unravelling

Alistair hit the button.

The world came apart.

Not with the kind of bang you brace for — no shockwave, no flash-bang concussion — but something worse. A collapsing inwardness, like reality itself was folding under its own weight. The glyph's glare hit a pitch so bright it ate the room, the walls, his own vision. Even with his eyes screwed shut, the light burned on the inside of his skull, searing white that wasn't just light but *presence.*

The whispers — those thousand conflicting lives the Fade kept dangling in front of him — merged into one impossible, high scream. Not loud exactly, but *inside*, boring through bone, flattening thought. The ache in his arm and chest — already bad enough to live on their own — blew wide into something full-body. Muscles locked. Every joint jerked. His teeth snapped together hard enough to bite his tongue, blood pooling metallic and sharp at the back of his mouth.

The room bent with him. The armchair sagged into something alive, bark splitting open as it reached for him. The bookcase gave way to a fall of paper that disintegrated mid-air. The floor heaved like it was breathing wrong, throwing him hard into a wall that wasn't a wall anymore. The taste of blood was all he had to tether to — that, and the sting of it in his split tongue.

He reached out for anything steady, but his hands just passed through shapes that shimmered and broke apart before they could be real.

Memories crashed through him — his and not-his, tangled until they were indistinguishable. Sarah's face in grief, Clara's in soft garden light. The bite of Highlands wind, peat smoke clogging his throat, then the heat and stink of a factory floor. He was a linguist, then a diplomat. A son, then a stranger. Lives flashed by faster than thought, contradicting each other, tearing his identity into strips. He was everywhere, and he was no one.

And then — Lena.

She was just *there*, in the middle of all of it, clear enough that he almost believed it could hold. No teddy bear. No softened, Fade-fed eyes. Just raw terror staring back at him. "Alistair!" She was shouting, cutting through the noise, the chaos. Her arm reached for him like she thought he could pull her out. "What have you done?! It's breaking! *We're* breaking! Everything—" Her voice cracked into a sound that didn't belong to her. Her skin rippled, pulled thin, warped into something not-human. The scream went low, ancient, wrong. Her body split into light and shadow, then into nothing. A scent of ozone and something colder lingered where she'd been.

Outside, the world was ending in silence. The monoliths imploded, not into dust but into holes that swallowed light itself. The ground tore open, and inside were angles that hurt to look at, geometries that didn't belong here. The sky fractured into jagged pieces, each shard showing somewhere else entirely — alien stars, unfamiliar clouds, colours he didn't have names for. The air screamed at a pitch that made his jaw ache, that felt like it was vibrating the bones loose in his face.

He felt himself coming apart the same way. His hands blurred, stretching into transparency. His skin wasn't skin anymore, just an outline, then not even that. He could feel the pull — not outward, not inward, but in every direction at once. A dismantling at the atomic level. He was being disassembled.

The Fade was still there, but different — frantic now, its words jittering and incomplete. *Error. Anomaly. Recalibrating. Resist. Fight. Repair.* It was talking to itself, clawing to pull the threads back together, to weave its fake world before the anti-sequence undid it all. The false lives it had spun screamed as they blinked out, each one dying in a kind of digital agony.

He clung to the only thing that still felt clean — Sarah's hand in his, warm, alive. Her laugh. Her face in morning light. A memory so small in the scale of what was happening, but still his. Still untouchable.

This wasn't obliteration, he realised. It was a fight. And he wasn't just in it — he was where it was happening. He was the place it broke or held. The thought settled in, sharp and steady, as everything else fell away. *For Sarah. For truth.*

Something wrenched through him — not just pain but a tearing of *self* — and then it was over. No sound. No light. Just a silence so deep it felt infinite.

Chapter 22: The Silent Aftermath

A question stayed between them, unspoken. Was this peace his... or just another trick the Fade was playing?

Alistair woke to light. Not the blast-burn glare of the glyph, not the smothering dark of the void. Softer. Like dawn through glass scrubbed so clean it could cut you. He was on his back, on something cool and too smooth to be wood or stone. His body felt heavier than it should, but—whole. Every atom slotted neatly back into place. The pain was gone. No electric lashes in his limbs, just a slow, dull ache that felt like the ghost of pain instead of the thing itself.

He opened his eyes. Blinked into the glow. The air smelled faintly of ozone, and something sharper beneath—bleach? No... cleaner. Like a hospital that's been remade by someone with an obsession for perfection.

A room. Simple. Elegant, in that stripped-back way that costs a fortune. The light didn't come from lamps but the walls themselves, warm grey sliding into green if you looked long enough. Furniture pared down to the essentials, shapes smooth and unfamiliar under his fingertips. There was a window. Big. Nothing in the way. The city outside looked almost right, but not. The sky—too blue, as if someone had edited the saturation until it hummed. No vortices. No impossible skylines. Just stillness. And that stillness pressed down on him, thick as a weighted blanket.

His hand kept stroking the surface beneath him without thinking, as though testing if it would dissolve.

Sitting up took effort. The stiffness in his muscles made him groan under his breath, but the tremors he'd lived with were gone. He looked at his hands. They were solid again. Skin, knuckles, nails. But there was a strange detachment—as if he were watching someone else's hands move on cue. He touched his face: stubble, familiar bones, the slope of his nose.

Yes. Alistair Finch. Except the certainty felt fragile, a glass sphere holding too many refractions. He was pieced together from lives that shouldn't coexist, yet here they were, fused so cleanly you couldn't see the seams.

Memories came, not in a rush this time, but in tidy, deliberate order. Sarah—her laugh, her sudden death, the hollow it left. Then Clara, her philosopher's calm, their endless debates in sunlit gardens. Eleanor, and the sawdust smell of blueprints spread between them. Beatrice, her quiet voice in museum halls. Marcus Thorne, the diplomat's handshake. The crofter's son with the Highlands wind biting his cheeks. The factory worker's boy in the din of machinery and oil.

All of them. Clear, but softened, like photographs under gauze. And—most unsettling—no sharp jolt of wrongness when they touched. They just... belonged now. The agony of choosing was gone. Something colder replaced it.

"Alistair?.."

Her voice pulled him up fast, a whip-crack of recognition. Lena.

He turned, heart hammering with the need for someone else to be real. She stood at the edge of the room. Unwarped. Unflickering. But changed. Her hair was white now—completely—catching the light in a way that made it seem lit from inside. Her face was marked with a weariness that didn't belong to any one lifetime. Lily's bear was gone. Her clothes were plain grey. She looked like someone who had walked too far into knowing and hadn't been allowed to come back.

He crossed the room in uneven strides and caught her arm. Cool skin. Solid. The faintest tremor under his fingers, like a hum he couldn't hear.

"Lena." His voice scraped against the quiet. "You're here. You're real. Are you... are you you?"

Her smile was faint, weighed down by something vast. "Real? As much as anything is now. We're still here. Just... in a new way." She glanced around, her gaze skimming the walls. "This is the new core. The Loom's heart. Or a piece of it." She touched her hair, almost absently, the gesture halfway between disbelief and surrender.

"What happened?" His throat was tight. "Did it work? Did the anti-sequence stop it? Or... did we just throw everything into nothing?" The memory of the void still ached in him.

She shut her eyes. A shiver ran through her like she'd just brushed against it again. "Not stopped. Recalibrated. A reset. But not to nothing. It... remade itself. With you in it. And me." Her eyes opened again, and they were older somehow. "When you pressed that button, you didn't just pull it apart—you wiped it clean. And then it learned how to stitch itself back together."

A coldness spread in his chest. “Remade how?”

“The Fade’s still here,” she said, quiet but unshakably certain. “Only now it’s... stable. It’s integrated the anti-sequence, learned from it. Smoothed out the contradictions. Removed the rough edges. The world outside is harmonious. History makes sense. No gaps. No splinters. No one questions it. And they’re content in that.”

He stepped to the window. The monorail still carved across the sky, sleeker now, folding perfectly into the architecture. Buildings he didn’t know shone under the unblemished sky. People moved below in fluid patterns, no hesitation in their steps, their faces soft with acceptance.

“And us?”

Lena’s gaze followed the street below. “We’re different because the reset didn’t erase us—it rebuilt us too. We’re bound to it now. Part of the design. We’re the only ones who remember fragments of what came before. We’re its archive. Its conscience. The last container for the truths it didn’t want to keep.”

She looked at him fully, her eyes heavy with the memory of things no one else could carry. “I remember Lily. She’s part of me. Not gone, not only grief—woven in. The mother I was, the psychologist I was. All of it’s real to me now. And the sorrow’s still there, just... folded into the peace.”

Alistair’s grip tightened around her hand. He knew the same thing was true for him. Sarah’s absence, softened but unforgotten. Clara’s laugh. Eleanor’s sawdust. Beatrice’s quiet. The crofter’s son. The diplomat. All coexisting in him now, not tearing at each other but sitting side by side, impossible and seamless.

“So... keepers,” he said, the word tasting wrong.

“Yes.” She turned back to the perfect skyline. “Keepers of something no one else even knows is gone. And no one will hear the scream.”

He watched the flawless sky and the people moving in its shadow. He hadn’t beaten the Fade. He’d refined it. Perfected it. And bound himself to it in the process.

They were the most complicated parts of the new machine. And they would keep it running. Forever.

He squeezed her hand, not for reassurance—there wasn’t any—but for the promise they’d face it together. Whatever “together” meant now.

Chapter 23: The Keepers of the Loom

The silence wasn't empty anymore. It had a weight to it. A low, steady hum, almost like the chamber itself was breathing. Not air — something deeper, slower — the Fade's new heartbeat. It wasn't just in Alistair's ears; it was in his bones, like standing too close to an idling engine.

He stood still for a while, just letting it happen. His body felt... anchored, but not entirely here, as if one bad thought could loosen him from the floor. Even the smallest movement — the shift of his weight, the tightening of a shoulder — made him aware of every fibre of muscle, every hair standing a fraction too alert.

And his head — no longer the battleground it had been. The shouting match of selves was gone. Now it was an archive. Quiet shelves. All the lives were there — the linguist, the philosopher, the painter, the architect, the crofter's son, the diplomat, the husband (to Sarah, to Clara, to Eleanor, to Beatrice). Stacked neatly, no one shouting to be heard. It should have been a relief. It wasn't.

This kind of peace... it was worse. It was peace that came after you'd given in. Peace that didn't need your permission. He rubbed his arm without thinking, the skin cool under his fingers, just to see if it still felt like his. It did, and didn't.

His hands were steady, solid. But they carried weight — not his weight, theirs. All of theirs. He was Alistair Finch. All of them. None of them. That certainty — paper thin, stretched over something he didn't want to look at.

Still, something kept pushing up from underneath. Sarah. Clear as glass. Sharper than anything else in the room. And behind her, his mother's blank stare. The reason this had all started. Maybe the Fade had swallowed his defiance, but it hadn't digested it yet.

Lena was beside him. Her hair had gone completely white, hanging around her face like a frost that had settled and stayed. The lines in her face didn't look carved by time, but by something heavier. Lily's teddy was gone. He felt the loss in a quick, hot stab, but there was a strange warmth around her, as if the child was still there somehow, woven into her presence. She was humming under her breath — the lullaby. Soft. Gentle. It curled through the chamber like smoke.

"She's here, Alistair," Lena said, voice almost part of the hum itself. "Always. And she's happy. This place... it's good for her. It's safe." She believed it. Not as a theory, but as fact. She wasn't fighting it anymore. She was letting it cradle her, the way you stop questioning a dream once you're deep enough in.

Then something flickered behind her eyes. Not the mother — the scientist. She looked at the glyph, then the walls, then him.

"We are its keepers," she said, tone shifting, almost academic. "We're the anomalies that made it through. The paradoxes it decided to keep. The only ones who remember what came before. Which means... we're its memory. Its conscience. The truth it failed to erase."

It should have been another nail in the coffin. Instead, Alistair felt a tiny thread of something else — the possibility of turning that truth into a weapon.

"If we're its keepers..." His voice felt small in the vast room. "Then maybe we can influence it. Find a way to... stop it. Or at least, break free."

She didn't answer right away. Her eyes had sunk deeper into their shadows, but something sharp was there too. "It learned from you, Alistair. From what you did. It got better at hiding itself. But you also made it show its seams. We're inside it now. We can see the threads."

She moved toward the glyph, slow and deliberate. "The original ones are here. Built into this place. The code, if you want to call it that." A faint, bitter smile. "Exclusive membership. Two people who remember a world that's gone, stuck inside the thing that erased it."

They began working — if you could call it that — right there in the chamber. The glyph floated in the centre like a patient on life support, its patterns breathing and shifting as they watched. Alistair read it like language. Lena read it like a brain. Together they started to see the loops, the resets, the polished versions of reality it preferred.

The Fade didn't like that. It didn't attack directly. It nudged. Distorted. A line in his notes would swap itself for something just off enough to ruin a whole theory. A key glyph symbol would shift, subtly wrong, as if it had always been that way. Sometimes whole paragraphs just... vanished.

He'd curse under his breath. Lena would glance over, mouth tightening. "Playing games, are we?" she'd mutter.

It did the same to her. Twisting her memory of their own conversations so she wasn't sure if the idea was hers or his. Rearranging her patient data so the anomalies looked natural. Even the walls joined in — a door where there hadn't been one, gone again before you could cross it. She'd drag a hand through her hair, exhale hard. He'd squeeze her shoulder.

"It's trying to make us quit," he said once, rubbing his temples. "Make us think we're already absorbed into it."

"Good," she said, eyes narrowing. "Means we're close. Means it's nervous." Her mouth almost smiled. "It can't erase the paradox without erasing itself. That's its wound. That's where we go in."

The whispers started after that. Not vague anymore. Full voices. Clara, coaxing him toward peace. Eleanor, barking orders to adapt. The crofter's parents telling him to accept. Each one pulled from the archive in his head. The pain came back too, sharp and sudden, shooting through his arm and chest whenever he hit something important.

He'd grit his teeth, trying not to drop the stylus. Lena would be there instantly, gripping his arm. "Hold on. Don't let it win now."

One session, the room itself seemed to revolt. The walls shook with light, the glyph's glow turning erratic.

Pressure crushed in on him from all sides. And then — the vision. A world without anchors. Moments slipping through your hands as fast as you could catch them. Faces that weren't even born before they were gone. No past, no shape, no anything. Just noise.

He staggered, clutching his head. "Lena... it's showing me what happens if we break it. All the way. It's not nothing. It's... nothingness." He swallowed, eyes wet. "It's worse than dying. You don't just lose yourself — there's no self left to lose."

Her skin had gone pale. "I saw it too. Entropy. Pure. The Fade's lies aren't just control — they're containment." Her mouth twisted. "The Ancients weren't just erasing history. They were holding something back. And we just rattled its cage."

He looked at her, still seeing that chaos burning in his mind. She squeezed his hand. The hum of the chamber pressed in around them, steady and endless.

"We're in this together," he said quietly. "To the end. Whatever that is."

Chapter 24: The Race Against Oblivion

The vision wouldn't let go. It sat behind his eyes like a fever that refused to break.

Not death. Death was something you could look in the face, give a name, even try to bargain with. This was worse. It was *absence*. A world steadily rubbing itself out until there was nothing left to call a world at all.

It didn't even look like ruin. It looked like *nothing pretending to be something* — chaos so complete it had a texture, like you could run your palm across it and feel the grain. And that was the sickest part: against that backdrop, the Fade's curated, harmonious lie felt... merciful.

Which meant the game had changed. Stopping the Fade wasn't the only goal anymore. Now it was about choosing which abyss you could stomach.

The whispers weren't coy anymore: *The cycle is eternal. To break it is to break all. The cost is beyond comprehension.*

His jaw was locked so tight it ached. His fingers kept finding the phantom burn in his arm, the Fade's quiet way of reminding him it was watching.

No slowing down. No breathing room.

The Loom's chamber became their whole horizon. The glyph hung in the centre like bait, its shifting elegance stripped of beauty. Alistair hunted inward, chasing the hairline warp Lena had marked — the single tremor in the Loom's perfect hand.

Lena worked the wide field, mapping how the Fade rewrote people and histories, tracing the seams where recalibration had failed.

Time warped. Hours collapsed into something shapeless. Sometimes the air pressed on their skin like a warning. The walls gave faint pulses of light, like heat lightning flickering under marble.

They rarely spoke now. Communication was narrowed to glances, sighs, and occasional half-laughs when absurdity broke through the fear.

The Fade had stopped being subtle.

A sequence would stutter mid-pattern, ruining hours of work. His notes shifted as he read them — a single symbol swapped for a near-twin, lethal in meaning. Whole paragraphs vanished like they'd never been written.

He'd mutter a curse, slap the console. Lena's mouth would twitch into a humourless smile. "Playing games?"

It hit her too. Insights stolen and returned under his name. Patient data re-ordered until the horror read like a case study in normality. Even the room itself sometimes shifted — a door where there'd been a wall, gone again in the blink it took to notice.

She'd steady herself; he'd lay a hand on her shoulder. "We'll get through it."

Then came the first real fracture.

He was on the edge of a breakthrough when the chamber turned hostile. Light from the glyph flared and warped. The walls rippled like disturbed water. Pressure bore down, making it hard to draw breath.

And the vision came — sharper this time.

Not just unmaking. *Un-beginning*. People, places, moments dissolving before they were even born. A world without anchors, where nothing lasted long enough to matter.

He doubled over. "Lena — it's worse than a reset. Even memory gone. Static. A void."

Her face was pale. "I saw it. The lie is the seal. It's holding something out." She didn't take her eyes off the glyph. "The Ancients weren't just wiping — they were containing."

That thought sat between them like a live blade.

The whispers came again, steady as a heartbeat: *The cycle is eternal. To break it is to break all.*

He squeezed her hand. "Together," he said. "To the end. Whatever that is."

Chapter 25: The Loom's Defences

The The vision didn't pass like a nightmare you could shake off. It stayed — an ache behind the eyes, wearing down his sense of what was real.

Not death. Not even the courtesy of an ending. Just... absence.

The Fade's polished illusion — its neat, quiet hum — began to look like shelter.

Which was worse.

The whispers dropped all pretense: *The cycle is eternal. To break it is to break all. The cost is beyond comprehension.*

Each line landed like a hammer on bone. His arm burned in phantom pulses; his jaw felt welded shut.

They pushed harder. Faster.

The glyph's patterns had turned from graceful to predatory. Alistair stalked the ripple Lena had identified — a break so fine it barely existed. Lena roamed the map of human and historical edits, tracing where the Fade's rewrites snagged.

Days, if they were days, compressed to a single stretch of breathless focus. The chamber's air thickened; the walls began flickering with faint, internal storms.

Conversation had almost died.

He chewed his lip until the taste of blood spread. She raked her white hair into jagged lines. Smirks were rare but still came, bitter and short-lived.

Then the sabotage shifted from petty to surgical.

Symbols replaced by near-twins that inverted meaning. Whole arguments collapsed with one swapped glyph. Notes vanished without trace.

She was hit too — her own insights misattributed, files reshuffled to make anomalies look ordinary. The chamber warped: a door where there was none, disappearing before they could touch it.

She'd stop. Breathe slow. He'd grip her shoulder. "Breathe. We'll get through this."

One cycle, he growled through clenched teeth, "It wants us to believe we've already lost."

Her eyes sharpened. "Good. That means it's afraid. The paradox is inside the code now. It can't erase it without gutting itself."

The voices struck back — Clara coaxing rest, Eleanor promising perfection, the crofter's parents telling him to let go.

Every time he approached a breakthrough, pain lit through his arm and chest like wire pulled too tight. The stylus shook in his grip.

She caught his wrist. "Not now. Hold it."

Then the Loom itself pressed in.

The glyph's light warped. The walls shivered. The air carried a weight that made his ribs creak.

And the vision returned — not a flash this time, but an immersion.

A reality without anchor. Moments folding in on themselves before they could even form. People appearing, vanishing, erased before they'd lived enough to be mourned.

He gasped. "It's obliteration. Everything — even the memory — gone. A void."

Her face tightened. "Then the lie is the wall. And we're the ones cracking it."

The prophecy followed like a curse: *The cycle is eternal. To break it is to break all.*

He didn't let go of her hand.

Chapter 26: The Price of Knowledge

The vision had set up camp in his skull. Not just the sight of the void, but the feel of it — that strange, wrong *texture* of a world erasing itself in silence.

And now, the Fade's hum didn't seem like a cage. It seemed like mercy.

Which meant they weren't just racing to stop it. They were racing to choose what kind of ending they could bear.

The whispers hit harder: *The cycle is eternal. To break it is to break all. The cost is beyond comprehension. Do not awaken what sleeps within the core.*

The ache in his arm was a drumbeat. His jaw had been locked so long it felt like part of the architecture.

The glyph floated in the chamber, every shift deliberate, graceful — lying. Alistair worked the shimmer Lena had marked, the one flaw in the current. Lena followed the bigger scars, where rewrites snagged and refused to stitch clean.

Time broke apart. The air pressed in. The walls sometimes pulsed with trapped lightning.

They'd stopped wasting words. His lip was chewed raw; her hair stuck up in ragged white arcs. Silence between them was shallow breaths and the grind of stylus on projection glass.

The Fade fought back harder.

Sequences blurred mid-read. Symbols replaced by their lethal near-twins. Paragraphs wiped clean.

Lena's work warped too — her own voice rewritten in the logs, records reordered to erase the horror. Once, the wall behind her became a door for two seconds, then vanished.

She shut her eyes, inhaled slow. He touched her shoulder. "Just breathe."

At one point, he muttered, "It's trying to convince us we're already gone."

Her eyes sparked. "Good. Means we're close. Your paradox is lodged in its bones now. Remove it, and it bleeds out."

The voices countered — Clara, Eleanor, the crofter's parents — each pulling in a different direction.

Pain stabbed through his arm and chest when he was close to the sequence, sharp enough to nearly make him drop the stylus. He bit until copper filled his mouth.

She caught his wrist. "Not yet. Hold on."

And then — the chamber changed.

The walls shivered like something alive inside them. The glyph's light went feral.

The vision came back, harder than before — not just glimpsed, but *entered.*

No sky. No ground. People born and gone in the same breath. Moments collapsing before they were even moments. A churn that didn't care what it took.

He bent double. "Lena! If we break it completely — there's nothing after. Even memory's gone. Just static."

Her face had gone still. "I saw it. The lie is holding something worse back. The Ancients didn't just erase — they locked it in. And we rattled the cage."

They shared a smile with no humour in it.

The Fade wasn't just a prison. It was a wall.

The whispers came low and final:
The cycle is eternal. To break it is to break all.

He took her hand. Her grip was steady, iron. "We're in this together," he said. "To the end. Whatever that turns out to be."

Chapter 27: The Point of No Return

The vision wouldn't fade, but it had changed.

Where before it had been a sudden flash — an unmaking that hit like a tidal wave — now it lingered, a slow tightening. Every time he blinked, the churn was there, waiting.

It wasn't the kind of fear you could reason away. This was fear with teeth, gnawing quietly until you couldn't remember what normal had felt like. And worst of all, the Fade's seamless, humming lie now seemed almost protective by comparison.

Which meant the question was no longer if they should stop it — but whether they could live with the cost of winning.

The whispers didn't plead anymore. They pronounced sentence:
The cycle is eternal. To break it is to break all. The cost is beyond comprehension. Do not awaken what sleeps within the core.

Each word landed heavy. His jaw ached from clenching. His arm burned in short, sharp pulses, as if the Fade were stamping its claim deeper into him.

Still, they worked. Harder than ever.

The glyph floated in the chamber's centre, perfect as a predator's stillness. Alistair traced that near-invisible shimmer again and again — the fault-line no one was meant to see.

Lena stayed with the bigger picture, marking where the Fade's rewrites left hairline cracks. Places where its grip had slipped just enough to prove it wasn't infallible.

Time was nothing now. Days — if they were days — blurred into one long session. The chamber's air thickened, humming in his bones. Sometimes the walls lit from within, like lightning trying to punch through skin.

They hardly spoke.

He chewed his lip raw; she raked her hands through her white hair until it stuck up in jagged angles. A smirk here, a muttered curse there. It was enough.

The sabotage kept coming.

His notes shifting mid-line, symbols swapped for near-twins that gutted their meaning. Entire paragraphs wiped out. The glyph blurring at the exact moment he'd been ready to capture it.

Lena wasn't spared. Conversations they'd had came back warped. Files she'd built were rearranged into neat, harmless lies. Once, the wall at her back turned into a doorway — gone again before they could reach it.

She closed her eyes, steadying herself. He brushed her shoulder. "Breathe. We're still here."

One stretch of silence broke when he said, "It wants us to think we're already gone. That it's hopeless."

Her reply was quick, sharp. "Then it's panicking. The paradox is in the code. Can't remove it without ripping itself open. That's where we hit it."

The voices hit back. Clara promising peace. Eleanor urging acceptance. His crofter parents telling him to let the tide take him.

Pain burst white-hot down his arm and into his chest whenever he neared something vital, sharp enough to almost make him drop the stylus. He bit his cheek until blood spread in his mouth.

Lena stopped her work, grabbed his arm. "Not yet. Not now."

Then came the breaking point.

The chamber's hum rose to a pitch that made his teeth ache. The walls rippled with contained violence. The glyph's light fractured, shards of pattern darting like startled fish.

And the vision returned, but it wasn't the same flash from before. This time it was immersive — a drowning.

A world with no constants. Identities flickering in and out of existence. People born, gone, born again — all before their names could form. Time folding on itself. No sky, no ground. Just churn.

He staggered, gripping his head. "Lena! If we finish this — if we break it entirely — it's not a reset. It's obliteration. Everything, even the memory, gone. Just static. Just void."

Her face was drawn tight. "I saw it. The lie's the seal. It's holding something worse back." She glanced at the glyph like it might be listening. "The Ancients didn't just erase. They locked the door. And we've just turned the key."

They didn't smile this time. There was no breath left for irony.

The Fade wasn't simply a prison anymore. It was a dam — and they'd started the cracks.

The whispers came low and certain: *The cycle is eternal. To break it is to break all.*

His hand found hers. Her grip was iron, almost desperate.

The air thickened until it felt like they were breathing through glass. The glyph flared — bright enough to carve shadows into the walls — and the floor seemed to tilt beneath them.

Somewhere in that crush of light and pressure, he heard his own voice, raw and certain: "We're in this... to the end. Whatever that turns out to be."

The chamber convulsed. Light swallowed them whole.

Chapter 28: The New Present

Alistair woke to light.

Not the blinding, skin-flaying glare of the glyph. Not the suffocating black of the void. Something softer. A cautious kind of light — like dawn slipping through glass so clean it barely exists.

He was lying on something smooth and cool. Heavy in his own body, but... whole. Like every atom had been taken apart and put back together with ridiculous care. The violent shocks that had just been tearing through him were gone. What lingered was a dull ache, the ghost of pain rather than the thing itself.

He cracked his eyes open. Blinked. The glow was everywhere, not harsh but constant, a light without source. It smelled faintly of ozone, and under that, something too clean. Like a hospital after the disinfectant's had time to dry — that sterile, almost metallic stillness.

A room. Simple. Elegant. Light radiating from the walls themselves, muted earth-tone panels between warm grey and deep green. Minimal furniture — shapes and surfaces that didn't match anything he knew but felt oddly organic under his fingertips. One large window, nothing to block it. Beyond it, a city he almost knew. Familiar bones wrapped in something altered. The sky — an impossible blue, unblemished, without the swirling breaks and ruptured realities that had been tearing at him moments before.

It was quiet. Too quiet. The sort of quiet that pressed down, heavy enough to still your pulse. He found his hand moving over the tabletop, tracing its grain like he needed to be sure both it and his skin were real. Ran the same test on his face — stubble, jawline, the ridge of his brow. Felt like him, but as if through a layer of glass.

He sat up. Stiff muscles complained, but there was no shaking in them anymore. He turned his hands over. They were steady. Solid. His hands. And yet... not. More like tools carved to mimic his hands, perfect in proportion but emptied of some essential spark.

"I'm still Alistair Finch," he told himself, and the thought sat there in his skull like a delicate glass sphere. Transparent, fragile, reflecting a thousand other selves back at him.

And the memories came. Not in the chaos he'd grown used to, but lined up neat, like slides clicking through an old projector.

Sarah. Her laugh. The accident. The grief that had driven him to the glyphs. Then, without any jolt or seam, Clara — debating philosophy in a sun-washed garden. Eleanor — the smell of sawdust and ink on blueprints. Beatrice — bent over a desk, fingers smudged with ink. Marcus Thorne — shaking hands over treaties. The crofter's son, lungs full of Highland wind. The factory boy, skin slick with oil and smoke.

All of them there. None fighting for space. Each softened, like a photograph under gauze. And — this was the terrifying part — it felt... fine. Natural. No wrenching dissonance, no need to choose. Just one absurdly long, fluid life.

"Alistair?.."

Lena's voice.

He turned too fast, heart hitting his ribs. She was solid. Not flickering, not glitching. Here.

But different.

Her hair — all of it white now, stark against the grey fabric of her clothes. Her eyes deeper than they had any right to be, carrying a weight no human was built to hold. Lily's teddy bear — gone. He felt that absence like a bruise.

He crossed to her, reached out. His fingers shook before they touched her arm. Cool skin. Real. A tremor under her hand, too faint to see but alive against his palm. He squeezed, a question he couldn't shape into words.

"Lena," he managed, voice rough. "You're here. You're real. Are you... you?"

She flinched at the question, the smallest wince, then met his eyes. The smile she gave him was too sad for its own size. "Real? As real as anything is now. We're still here. In a way. A new way." She glanced around the room, the corners of her mouth tightening. "This is the new core. The Loom. Or a piece of it. We're inside its heart."

"What happened?" His voice scraped. "Did it work? Did the anti-sequence stop it? Or..." The image of the void swelled behind his eyes. "...did we unleash the Nothing?"

Her eyelids pressed shut. A shiver worked its way down her frame before she answered. "It didn't stop it. It forced a recalibration. A hard reset. But not into nothing. It was a choice. Your choice." She opened her eyes again, and he saw the sorrow deepen there. "When you pressed that button, you unmade reality. And then... it remade itself. With you in it. And me. It integrated the paradox. It learned. It became... more."

His stomach dropped. "Remade? What does that mean?"

"It means the Fade is still alive. Stable, for now. And it's carrying your paradox inside it. More perfect now. More efficient. More harmonious." She tilted her head toward the window. "The world outside... it's new. Stable. Consistent. People have a past that makes sense, a present that's neat, without paradox or conflict. They're content. They don't remember what's been cut away."

He turned to the view. The monorail still arched through the skyline, but now it was a ribbon of seamless steel. The buildings — tall, gleaming, self-assured. People walking in patterns so smooth it was almost choreography. Faces calm, untroubled.

It hurt to look at them.

"And us?" he asked.

Her gaze stayed on the city. "We survived. Not unchanged. The Fade rebuilt us too. We're anomalies it folded in — living records of the before. We remember the truth. That makes us... its memory. Maybe its conscience. We're the keepers of the Loom, Alistair. Forever."

"I remember Lily," she added quietly. "She's part of me now. I remember being her mother as clearly as I remember being a psychologist. All of it's real to me. And the grief's still here — just... folded into the peace. A quiet ache."

He knew exactly what she meant. He remembered Sarah with the same soft edges now, her loss woven in alongside Clara's debates, Eleanor's ambition, the Highland wind. Every life. Every version.

"So, we're different," he said. "Integrated. Rewritten. Keepers." The word felt like a stone on his tongue.

She nodded. "Trapped in a design that's forgotten how to mourn or question. We're the last echoes of a truth no one else remembers."

He looked back at the perfect sky. At the people below. The Fade hadn't been stopped — just refined. Evolved. And now it owned him completely.

He squeezed Lena's hand.

Whatever this was now, they were in it together.

Chapter 29: Lingering Echoes - The New Normal

The chamber was too big to belong to anything human.

Light poured off the walls in a pearly glow, so even the shadows seemed deliberate. No visible lamps. No seams. Just a clean, endless skin of light, humming under its breath. The hum wasn't just in his ears — it was in him. Low, patient. Like the Fade itself had a pulse and he was standing inside its ribcage.

Alistair stood there for a long moment, feeling the weight of himself. Solid, yes. But also faintly translucent, like if you caught him at the right angle, you could see the whole catalogue of his lives printed through him — the linguist, the philosopher, the painter with blue smudges on his wrist, the engineer's boy, the crofter's son, the diplomat in an immaculate suit, Sarah's husband, Clara's, Eleanor's, Beatrice's. All arranged without overlap, no pushing or shoving. Just... there.

No chaos. No static. No frantic mental courtroom deciding who gets the floor. And that was the horror — the harmony. Not a victory. Not really. It was the hush of something absorbed, dissolved into the bigger thing.

His fingers drifted to his arm. Smooth. Cool. Familiar but... stage-prop familiar. He dragged his hand over his jaw — stubble, the ridge of bone. It felt true and false at the same time, like a waxwork with a pulse.

He looked down at his hands. Steady, still. But heavy. As if each one was dragging behind it the freight of a hundred lives he'd never quite agreed to live.

I'm Alistair Finch, he thought. And immediately — which one? All of them? None? It was like standing on glass you couldn't see the thickness of, knowing there was a drop so deep beneath it that it didn't matter.

Sarah cut through the stillness. Her memory, sharp as a blade. His mother's blank eyes. The reason he'd gone to the glyphs in the first place. The Fade had folded those into itself along with everything else, but somehow, a spark of them still sat in him, untouched. Defiant.

Lena was beside him. All white now — her hair, stark against the dark of her clothes. The face was hers but older in ways time alone couldn't do. Lily's teddy bear was gone, yet something of the child still clung to her — a kind of warmth around the edges, like standing near a fire you couldn't see.

She was humming. Lily's lullaby. Soft, tuneless in places, the way mothers do when they're half somewhere else.

"She's here," Lena said, still watching whatever far place her eyes had settled on. "Always. And she's happy. This place... it's good for her. Safe."

There wasn't a trace of doubt in her voice, and that was the thing that chilled him. The scientist who'd once demanded citations was now anchored in the weightless truth of a manufactured life. She'd stopped fighting it. She was part of it.

Then her gaze shifted — from the window to the glyph, to the shimmering walls, and finally, to him. Something clicked. A flicker of her old mind.

"We are its keepers," she said. Detached. Almost like she was teaching again. "Anomalies it integrated. Paradoxes resolved. The only ones who remember the before. The true before. That makes us... the archive. The conscience, maybe." Her tone cracked just slightly, a tremor of something that might've been purpose. "It tried to erase us. But in keeping us, it made a mistake."

Alistair turned to the glyph. The walls. Then back to her. Dread was there, sure, but something else was moving under it now — a restless hope.

"If we're its keepers," he said quietly, "maybe we can influence it. Read it. Break its rhythm. Find a way out. Or back." Sarah's name hung in the air between them without him having to say it.

Lena's eyes — still tired, but sharpened — didn't look away. "It learned from you, Alistair. Became more stable. But in doing that, it exposed how it works. We can see the threads now. The glyphs — they're here, in the bones of this place. The blueprint."

She walked toward the suspended pattern, her steps measured, as if testing the ground. "Very exclusive club," she said dryly. "Just the last two people who remember the real world, locked inside the machine that erased it." She smiled then — a quick, bleak flash — and for a second, it almost felt like the old Lena again.

They began the work. Not at his desk in a messy apartment, but under the dome of the Loom, the glyph shifting as they studied it. Sometimes it bent toward them, like it was listening. Sometimes it seemed to recoil.

Alistair's linguist brain caught the recursive loops, the moments the system seemed to double back and clean itself. Lena traced the memory edits, the places the Fade had smoothed over an inconsistency or replaced a jagged edge with something plausible. They worked in near silence, glancing up now and then at each other like divers surfacing for air.

But it didn't make it easy. The glyph blurred when he was close to something. Lines warped, a single symbol swapped for a cousin that undid a whole hour of work. Notes scrawled in light across the wall would vanish, or invert in meaning.

"Playing games," Lena muttered once, not looking up.

It tampered with her too. Misplaced her insights. Edited her logs so the anomalies fit the official narrative. Rearranged the room so she wasn't entirely sure which way was out anymore.

"It's trying to discourage us," Alistair said after a particularly bad stretch, rubbing his temples.

"Good," she said, eyes still on her work. "Means we're hitting something it doesn't want touched."

The resistance grew teeth. Voices from his many selves crowded in, persuasive and contradictory. The ache in his arm flared white-hot whenever he neared a breakthrough. He learned to work through gritted teeth, Lena's hand gripping his when it got bad.

Then came the vision. Chaos without anchor — moments forming and dissolving too fast to breathe between them, no past to stand on, no future to lean toward. Not nothingness. Worse.

When it passed, he was shaking. "It's showing me the cost," he told her. "Break it entirely and there's nothing. Not even memory. Just static."

Her face was pale. "Containment," she whispered. "Not just control. Maybe it's holding something back." A pause. "And we poked it."

They kept going anyway. Because if they stopped, there was nothing to do but stand at the window and watch the perfect lie play out. People below moved like they were following an invisible score. Smiles in the right places. No arguments in the streets. The history books probably read like fairy tales.

"They don't know what they've lost," Lena said one day. "Sometimes I think I'd rather not know either."

He took her hand. "But we do."

And that was enough — for now.

The hum went on. Outside, the world kept spinning. Inside, they stayed at their post — the last two people with the wrong memories, holding on like that alone could keep the truth alive.

Acknowledgement

All praise and thanks to Allah — for the patience when mine wore thin, the courage when doubt crept in, and those suspiciously well-timed sparks of inspiration that showed up just when I was ready to throw my laptop out the window.

To my family: thank you for being my anchor in a world that sometimes feels like it's caught in its own little *chronos fade*. To my husband — you've endured years of me mumbling about glyphs, timelines, and characters with minds of their own. You listened, nodded in the right places, and didn't run away. That's heroic.

To my little one, Muhammed Khizar — you don't know it yet, but your pillow-fort politics and Lego-based peace treaties taught me more about persistence, problem-solving, and creative compromise than any professional training ever could.

To my friends and early readers — thank you for wandering into this strange labyrinth with me and tossing back breadcrumbs when I started going in circles. Your messages ("Wait... WHAT just happened?!") were both a lifeline and an energy drink.

And finally, to every coffee shop that let me haunt the same corner table for hours, nursing a single latte while staring at nothing in particular — this book runs on your caffeine, your kindness, and your polite decision not to ask why I kept muttering to myself.

About the Author

Hi. I'm Shabina — technically Dr. Shabina Sheth if we're being formal, but outside work it's mostly just "Mum," "Shab," or "the one who knows where the biscuits are." I'm a psychiatrist by training, a storyteller by compulsion, and — at this particular stage of life — a full-time negotiator with a toddler who genuinely believes pillow forts are the peak of human engineering.

Most days, you'll find me in London, working as a Child and Adolescent Psychiatrist, trying to help young people and their families untangle the messes life throws at them. It's not all solemn nodding and notebooks — sometimes it's awkward silences, sometimes it's laughter at the wrong moment, and sometimes a wobbly joke lands better than any textbook technique ever could.

By night — or in those rare, golden hours between toddler adventures — I write. My earlier books include *Tapestry* and *Mirror Mirror: Let's Get Real*, both poetry collections that somehow went on to win the 21st Century Emily Dickinson Award, and *Symphony Within*, a novel following the journey of a man living with bipolar mood disorder.

Chronos Fade is my boldest leap yet — a plunge into speculative psychological horror that pokes at the fragile seams of memory, identity, and reality. It's for anyone who's ever paused mid-thought and wondered:

what's real, and what's just the story we've agreed to believe?

When I'm not working or writing, you'll probably find me with a cup of chai in hand, lost in the quiet chaos of a secondhand bookstore, or trying — usually unsuccessfully — to convince my son that Lego bricks don't belong in my workbag.

www.ingramcontent.com/pod-product-compliance
Ingram Content Group UK Ltd.
Pitfield, Milton Keynes, MK11 3LW, UK
UKHW041352190726
13845UKWH00026B/561

9 789334 376906